AF423208

THE FLAMINGO'S FATED MATE

ELVA BIRCH

Copyright © 2022 by Elva Birch

All rights reserved.

No part of this book may be reproduced in any form or by any electronic or mechanical means, including information storage and retrieval systems, without written permission from the author, except for the use of brief quotations in a book review.

For April Fool's, I enjoy harmless pranks, like mocking up fake covers and blurbs. Sometimes, these backfire on me beautifully, and in this case, I have never had so much demand for a book I swore I wasn't going to write.

After about a year of "not writing" this book, I'm so happy to bring you Frank and Anita's story.

Thank you to my readers for the flamingo memes and all the encouragement. This would never have happened without you.

You're a terrible influence and I love you!

LAWN ORNAMENT SHIFTERS

This is the book I swore I wasn't writing, ever since I mocked up a cover for April Fool's 2021. The joke was on me, of course, and this has been my most demanded title ever since. Now at last: the flamingo jokes! The Simon Says game where Anita makes Frank stand on one leg forever! The cupcakes! The cuddles!

Short, hilarious, and full of heart, fall in love with the quirky characters who run Wilson Kinetics, world famous artists and lawn ornament manufacturers. Shifters meet their fated mates in these clever, quick-paced stories of adventure and romance, set in a world with shifters, gnomes, and more!

The Flamingo's Fated Mate (book 1)
Gnome Sweet Gnome (book 2)
A Bear in a Birdbath (book 3)
A Garden for a Gargoyle (not that I'm writing it…)

For sketched and signed paperbacks, audiobooks, and swag, visit my webpage: elvabirch.com!

CHAPTER 1

There were two thousand cupcakes in the back of Anita's van.

It was a lot of cupcakes.

Anita stared at the results of her labor over the last day and a long, sleepless night. There were boxes of cupcakes on every shelf and even in the aisle between them, each of them with tidy rows of lemon and mint, chocolate and cherry, vanilla and peach. Every cupcake was perfectly iced with an artistic swirl and topped with a tiny garnish and a little flag with her bakery logo.

It was six in the morning and just starting to snow. Anita's wrists ached and her back had a warning twinge that reminded her that she wasn't twenty anymore; bending over pastries with a piping bag was harder work than it looked.

It was hours and hours before the charity event started and there were no other vehicles at the back loading dock where Anita had been instructed to bring the cupcakes. She had a moment of worry that no one was going to be there yet to let her in, but she'd always rather be early than late, and this was her opportunity of a lifetime.

Today, two thousand of the city's biggest muckety-muck businesspeople were going to be eating *her* cupcakes, and staring at *her* branding, while they emptied their pockets for charity and rubbed elbows with the other elite and upper class at the Wild and Wet Charity Gala.

It was the kind of thing that could make or break a little bakery like hers, and she wasn't going to blow it by being late because the weather was bad.

And it was *dramatically* bad.

Anita frowned up into the snow and wondered if she should wait until she made contact with the event coordinator before she started actually carrying boxes in. The loading dock had a little overhang protecting it, but it was windy and she didn't want the boxes to get wet with snow.

She closed the van door and climbed up the ramp to the little man door next to the big rolling doors for unloading semis. Her first knock was timid, but she leaned into the next one. She wasn't going to get anywhere in life if she didn't take chances.

There was no answer, so Anita put her hand on the handle and pulled. Just as she decided it was locked, it sprang open with a clang and she went staggering back.

The janitor on the other side of the door looked as surprised as she was, but as soon as Anita caught her balance, she was quick to say, "Oh, thank goodness! Don't let the door close! I have two thousand cupcakes that need to go inside *right now*, and it's starting to snow!"

"C-cupcakes?" the man stuttered, staring at her. He was handsome enough, but seemed a little slow.

"Cupcakes," Anita repeated. "Tiny little cakes with frosting. Hold the door, please!"

She scampered back to her van and wrenched the back

door open, pulling the first two half-sheet boxes carefully from the floor and bumping the door closed again with her hip. As fast as she could, she was back at the loading dock, carrying in the cupcakes. The man followed her bemusedly inside, and Anita looked around. There was a kitchen to the right and a long, dark hallway that must lead to the ballroom. No one else was there yet.

"Do you know where these should go?" she asked the janitor.

He gazed at her a moment and she repeated, "The cupcakes. Where should I put the cupcakes?"

"The kitchen?" the janitor guessed.

"The kitchen," Anita said kindly. "Good idea." The kitchen was enormous, probably three times the size of her entire bakery, and shiny with chrome. The janitor turned the lights on and Anita put her bakery boxes on the nearest counter. "I've got to get the rest of them in here before the snow gets any worse!"

She left him struggling with a doorstop for the outer door and got a second armload, passing him as she came back up the ramp. Together, they unloaded box after box, hurrying as the snow came down thicker and thicker. The janitor found a wheeled cart, and they stacked it as high as they dared and pushed it together up the ramp through the gathering slushy snow.

By the time they brought in the last boxes, the snow was ankle-deep and her van looked like it had been covered in a fluffy blanket.

"That's it, then," Anita said with relief, as they stacked the final cupcakes. "We made it, all eighty-four boxes. Thank you so much for your help." She cheerfully offered the janitor her hand to shake, and he did, holding onto it considerably longer than she expected him to, as shy as he'd been.

"I'm Anita," she said with a grin. "I own Donut Worry, Be Happy." She laughed at herself, feeling punchy and exhausted. "I say *own*, but really, I'm the whole thing. Just me."

"I'm Frank," the man said, smiling slowly. "That's a lot of cupcakes. You made them all yourself?"

"It was a lot of work," Anita admitted, finally taking her hand back and realizing that she had dyed her fingertips with pink food coloring. "I haven't slept."

"I'm really sorry," Frank said.

Anita rubbed her throbbing wrist. "It was worth it," she said with satisfaction. "This is my big chance. The kind of thing that could launch my bakery to greatness, you know? It was crazy of me even to apply. I thought for sure that Harriet Slade at Patty Cakes would get it, but I had to try, anyway. You've got one life to live, my mother always said. And now, not only can I pay the rent, but Frank Wilson the gazillionaire and all these really important people are going to eat *my* cupcakes and see *my* dorky name. It's probably the most exciting thing that has ever happened to me!"

Frank was still sort of staring at her like he couldn't quite help himself, but Anita wasn't sure if that could be blamed on his mental state. She was kind of babbling, and she could come across a little strong even when she had gotten a good night's sleep.

He winced. "No, I'm *really* sorry," he explained. "The charity event was canceled."

It was Anita's turn to stare. "Canceled?" she squeaked. "It was *canceled?*"

"There's a giant snowstorm blowing in. We're supposed to get three feet by the afternoon and they're already warning that the power might go out when the wind hits. Didn't you get the cancellation notice?"

Anita felt a wave of despair. "How was it sent? I've been kind of busy making two thousand cupcakes, and I haven't had a chance to check my email. I forgot my phone at home."

"Didn't you hear the news? There's a travel advisory on every channel!"

"Two *thousand* cupcakes!" Anita protested.

"I am *so sorry,*" Frank said, and he seemed to be taking it really personally for a janitor.

"I'm sure it's not your fault," Anita said unhappily. "It was just...my big *chance*. And what am I going to do with two thousand cupcakes?"

"I'll still pay you for them," Frank said firmly.

Anita, who had been looking at the food coloring stains on her fingers, looked up at him in alarm as the details finally snapped into place in her tired mind. Frank the janitor. Like Frank Wilson. "You're—"

"Frank Wilson, the gazillionaire," he said sheepishly.

And all the lights in the building went out.

CHAPTER 2

It actually took Frank a moment to realize that the power in the building had gone out. His flamingo was certain that the light in the world had simply gone away because they had caused their mate such bitter disappointment.

His flamingo had woken him frantically and driven him into the quickest clothing to hand—the jeans and stained shirt he wore to work on machinery. *Flock! Flock!* his flamingo kept shrieking, and that had made it very hard to think indeed when he met the adorable, plucky little baker who put him to work carrying cupcakes under the assumption that he was some kind of janitor.

She was his mate, he realized. His one true love. He'd always doubted the concept, figuring it was a comfortable fiction for people unwilling to put work into a relationship. But one look at her sparkling brown eyes, and he and his flamingo were both lost.

And then he'd offered her money, like that would solve everything.

Fix it fix it fix it, his flamingo was insisting now.

Anita squeaked in the darkness and Frank reached forward for her automatically and caught her arms reaching out for him. Her touch was like an electric shock as they grasped each other by the forearms and held on, waiting for the lights to come back.

Snuggle, his flamingo suggested, but Frank knew that would be too forward of him.

Snuggle! his flamingo repeated.

"Don't you have a generator or something?" Anita asked when it became apparent that the lights weren't going to come right back on.

"I have no idea," Frank said. "I just rented this place."

"Well, do you have a flashlight?" she asked practically. "The last thing I want to do is run into a pile of cupcake boxes."

Frank wracked his brain. Probably this wasn't the kind of kitchen to have a junk drawer full of useful things like that. "My phone!" he exclaimed. He had to let go of one of her arms in order to reach into his pocket and was gratified that her other hand seemed to hold on to him harder. Was she afraid of the dark?

He found his phone and fumbled to turn it on one-handed and find the control for the flashlight. It wasn't much, in the big, dark kitchen, and jagged shadows fled before the beam. Anita stepped closer to him with a hiss of alarm. "Oh," she breathed. "It's actually scarier this way. I feel like I'm in a horror movie. Do you hear a bloody hook on the back door?" She laughed weakly. "Sorry, I talk too much and have too active an imagination."

Snuggle! Frank's flamingo was all but stomping his feet.

Frank wasn't actually averse to the idea of snuggling. He was, in fact, quite enamored of the idea. Anita was curvy and looked like she'd be a delight to hold in his arms.

"I can't believe the power is out!" she said, stepping tantalizingly close as he swung the beam of the flashlight around in the weirdly reflective kitchen. "I mean, bad enough that the event was canceled, and I'm probably stuck here all day because I'm not sure my van would make it through the snow, but now there's no power! And with you! Of all people! Oh no, I mean, not like that, I'm sure you're fine, and you're certainly *fine*, it's just…"

She put her hand over her face and Frank realized he'd just watched someone actually, physically, facepalm.

"I'm sorry, everyone is always telling me I have no editor, and it's apparently even worse when I haven't slept. I should always stop one sentence earlier."

"I rented the penthouse upstairs," Frank said.

"I am *not* that kind of girl," Anita said tartly, snatching her hand off of him. "You bought cupcakes, mister gazillionaire, not me."

It was Frank's turn to be flustered. "No, of course not. I didn't mean, no, never, definitely not."

"Well, you don't have to be *that* sure," she muttered, just as Frank realized he'd said it much more firmly than courtesy dictated.

It was hard to think around Frank's flamingo, who was still stuck on the snuggle idea, and besides that, was pretty sure that the way to her heart was through dancing. If there was one thing Frank knew, it was that he was completely making a hash of this introduction and that bobbing his head and flapping his elbows was very unlikely to improve matters.

"Look, this has all gone terribly sideways," he said honestly. "Can I just start over?"

Anita looked at him suspiciously. "Like, we've just met, and you weren't pretending to be the janitor?"

"I never pre—yes, let's do that. Let's say that I was never a janitor and you've just arrived. 'Hello, Miss…?'"

Anita giggled cautiously. "Townsend," she supplied.

"'Hello, Miss Townsend, welcome to the Wild and Wet Charity Gala, which, while we're pretending, hasn't been canceled. I'm Frank Wilson, the gazillionaire, and I've hired you only for your cupcakes.'"

Snuggle, his flamingo muttered.

CHAPTER 3

nita was surprised by how strong and confident Frank's second handshake was, given that he sometimes looked like he was having an argument with someone in his head...and was losing. She was really glad for the touch, though, because the dark kitchen and the weirdly quiet building were making anxiety and terror swell in her, undoubtedly exacerbated by being sleep-deprived and half-starved.

She held onto his hand longer than she meant to and then let go rather sharply and felt adrift in the darkness. "It's really spooky," she blurted. Remembering their charade, she quickly added, "'I mean, I am so pleased to be here, Mr. Wilson. What a delightful party you throw! Such excellent taste in cupcakes!'"

"It's probably lighter in the ballroom," Frank suggested in his real voice. "All those big windows will let in any daylight that there is." He cleared his throat. "'Would you like to accompany me to the party in a very non-penthouse sort of way, Miss Townsend?'"

Anita took the janitor-celebrity's offered arm and

strolled with him down the hallway towards a room that opened up only slightly less black and more gray. It was dark outside for the hour, and blowing snow obscured the view of the river. "'It's a lovely day for a charity ball, I believe,'" she said in a terrible British accent. "'Not snowing at all!'"

"'I ordered the very best weather with my gazillion dollars,'" Frank said seriously. "'May I offer you refreshment?'" They stopped at a folding table clad only in a white tablecloth and he poured her a drink in an imaginary glass from an imaginary bottle.

"'I'm charmed!'" Anita declared, accepting it. They toasted each other and pretended to drink. "'I understand you have purchased only the most delectable foods and beverages. Such a swanky event. What a crowd! Look at all these famous people!'"

"'I hear the host is something else though,'" Frank said, straight-faced and snotty-voiced. "'He pretended to be a janitor, can you imagine?'"

"'Shocking!'" Anita giggled. "'Shall we mingle?'"

Frank offered his elbow again and Anita thought it wasn't too forward to snuggle rather close to him. It was, after all, a little chilly in the drafty room.

"'Oh, there's the mayor,'" he said, suddenly steering Anita in another direction. "'He's campaigning again and wants me to endorse him. Let's go hide behind these people or he'll talk your ear off. That's the chief of police, but that's definitely *not* his wife.'"

Anita played along. "'I see Victoria Hennings, the TV anchor. She didn't let me park in her spot once. I had to carry seventeen cakes almost a block. Let's snub her.'"

"'I hate her forever,'" Frank promised. "'I'll never watch her morning show again.'"

"'Oh no,'" Anita cried, clutching his arm. "'That's Harriet Slade. Hide me!'"

Frank was happy to let her duck to his far side and press up against him as they walked.

"Who is Harriet Slade?" he asked, forgetting his voice. "I mean, 'Who on earth is Harriet Slade?'"

"'Harriet Slade is my arch-nemesis, of course.'"

It was hard to believe that someone as adorable and cheerful as Anita had an arch-nemesis. "'Has she threatened your family honor?'" Frank asked, miming a sword at his waist.

"'Nothing so common,'" Anita said with impressive snootiness. "'We are *cupcake* rivals.'"

Frank let his imaginary sword go. "'I did not realize that baking was so competitive,'" he confessed.

"'She owns the Patty Cakes chain of bakeries downtown and my store is quite new and apparently rather threatening.'" Anita raised her chin and tipped her head like they were passing another couple. "'The cupcake business is quite cutthroat!'"

"'Shall I have security throw her out?'" Frank offered in a whisper.

Anita giggled. "'I don't suppose that will be necessary,'" she said. "'But perhaps you could have her car towed? She has a very fancy car.'"

They had circled the room and were at a low stage that had a weird collection of shapes draped in cloth. In the muted light from the window, they looked like cheap Halloween ghosts.

"Would you like to see the latest of my sculptures?" Frank had dropped his fancy voice and actually sounded shy.

Anita knew that Frank Wilson's fame and fortune had come, in a non-linear way, from lawn ornaments. His outdoor, articulated metal sculptures had been art collectors' items at first, selling for hundreds of thousands of dollars apiece at auction. He'd shot to greatness, quickly becoming a celebrity in exclusive art circles.

He had shocked the art world when he declared that he was going to start mass-producing the pieces and he bought up an abandoned car plant in the city and employed factory workers at union rates to make smaller, simpler versions from recycled parts and scraps.

Critics swore he would bankrupt himself and devalue his sculptures, but the market turned out to be surprisingly receptive and the Wilson Kinetic line of home decoration had skyrocketed him into riches and recognition. Every year since, he unveiled two versions of a new design—a large and complicated sculpture that he auctioned for a charity of his choice, and a smaller home version that would be generally affordable and available throughout garden shops across the country and in parts of Canada.

"'I'd be delighted to see it,'" Anita said in her best snooty voice. "'I'm considering purchasing it with my cupcake money.'"

"'I don't know, it might cost penthouse money,'" Frank said skeptically, with a sly, sideways look. "'The bidding can get very high…'"

Anita pretended to choke on her imaginary champagne and glared at him as long as she could keep from laughing—which wasn't very long.

"I'm glad you thought that was funny," he said, with his authentic voice full of relief.

"I'm pretty punch drunk," Anita admitted. "I was up all night making cupcakes, so everything is funny." Then she leaned close to confess in a whisper, "Okay, no, I'm this much of a dork all the time. I can't blame it all on the cupcakes."

Frank had really nice teeth, bright in the dim light, and a genuine smile. "I won't tell," he promised just as quietly, looking around like their pretend audience might overhear. "'Oh, it's time for the big reveal. It's my moment of fame!'"

Anita clapped loudly and turned to hush imaginary people. "'Quiet in the peanut gallery! The gazillionaire is going to uncover all the big metal stuff! Stuff it, Victoria Hennings!'" She turned back to Frank. "You're up, stud. Knock 'em dead."

Frank sprang to the stage, waving and blowing kisses to all the people that weren't actually there. He started to speak several times, play-acting that there was too much applause to continue. Anita clapped until her palms stung, whistling and hooting. It was absurd in the empty, echoing room, but then, everything about this day already was and it could only be about seven in the morning.

"'Without further ado, I give you this year's Wilson Kinetic Sculpture!'" Frank yanked the sheet aside and Anita froze in wonder.

She's seen photos of his work—who hadn't?—but there was nothing quite like seeing something like this in person. It was larger than she thought it would be, and much more intricate.

"It's supposed to be lit up," Frank said nervously, as Anita realized she'd stopped clapping. "It should have colored lights from there, and there, and there would be music, of course. Some kind of loud march. It would all be very impressive."

Anita clambered up onto the stage. "It's a flamingo!" she exclaimed in joy.

CHAPTER 4

Frank had unveiled a lot of Wilson Kinetic Sculptures by now, but he had never been as invested in the audience as he was in this one. The critics he'd been desperate to impress, the investors he'd been frantic to woo...none of them mattered even a fraction as much as his mate. The delight in her glowing face was the reward he hadn't even known he was craving.

"I thought it was appropriate," he said shyly. "For a lot of reasons…"

"Well sure," Anita said eagerly. "You have a lawn ornament business. How could you not have a flamingo in the line? Will you…?" She flapped her hands eagerly.

Frank reached up and pulled on the crank, not taking his eye from Anita for even a moment. He watched her squeal in glee as the wings fluttered and the neck snaked down and back up gracefully. One leg extended and tucked back up. Lapping metal feathers shivered down the back. The clockwork was so smooth it barely made a sound, just a ticking rustle as the pieces whispered together. The mechanism took only the tiniest amount of pressure, all so perfectly balanced and counterweighted that it continued going for several minutes after he let go.

Rose quartz and pink topaz gemstones were set in several places, and even in the non-ideal lighting, it glimmered and flickered.

Anita crowded close, clinging happily to him as she watched its dance. "It's amazing!" she said, almost sounding choked. "I've never seen anything so wonderful in my life!" Then she looked up at him in awe, and Frank had never seen anything so wonderful in *his* life.

This was it.

His purpose, his entire happiness, was here in the arms of this amazing woman. He'd been one of his own sculptures, moving through the motions of life on a mechanical track, act and counteract, waiting for some purpose to make him more than a machine.

And here she was, the vibrant, unstoppable woman who was his mate, with her forward, funny heart on her sleeve and her indomitable spirit obvious to anyone with eyes.

"'I bid one thousand dollars!'" she said loudly, raising her hand imperiously.

"Anita…"

"That's way, way too low, isn't it," she whispered back in her true voice. She was gazing at the flamingo sculpture again, still looking awed. "What should I start with? Like one hundred thousand? A million? I'm not letting Victoria Hennings outbid me."

"Anita, there's something I have to tell you…"

"It's for a good cause!" she protested. "I mean, I'll be in debt the rest of my life, but I'll have this gorgeous flamingo to make me happy, and it saves wildlife habitat, right?"

"Anita…" Frank could not help but chuckle.

"I suppose it comes with delivery for that price?" she asked anxiously. "I think it's too tall to fit inside my delivery van. Oh, maybe I can screw it onto the top like ice cream trucks have those giant cones! Oh, yes! It will be my new trademark look. People will buy my cupcakes just to get my van parked in front of their buildings for a little while. But what will that do to my car insurance? Do you think they'll hike up my premium because of the increased risk of theft? Of course, it will be hard to sneak that thing away. Oh no, what if it gets knocked off going under an overpass?"

"Anita!" Frank had to resist the urge to take her by the arms and kiss her to make her listen.

Anita put a hand over her face, giggling hysterically. "I'm sorry," she said sheepishly, peeking through her fingers. "Punch-drunk and hungry. Do you have, like, an energy bar or something? I think I'm going to crash really soon."

Feed her! Frank's flamingo insisted with a hiss.

"We have food!" Frank said instantly, for once in complete agreement with his inner animal. "In the kitchen. We've got all the hors d'oeuvres and two thousand cupcakes, and if we don't eat everything in the fridge it will go bad."

Anita snorted. "I know I'm a little fluffy, but I definitely cannot eat two thousand people's worth of hors d'oeuvres."

"I didn't mean that you'd have to eat it all!" Frank said, horrified that she'd think that was what he'd been trying to imply. "I just meant, don't feel bad for eating as much as you want."

It was dark down the back hallway to the kitchen, and Anita clung delightfully to his arm. Frank was distracted by how warm she was against his side, and how good she smelled, like sugar and lemons.

"Did you ever think about how hors d'oeuvres is spelled?" she chattered. "I mean it doesn't look a thing like it sounds. I must have been in college before I realized that it wasn't pronounced whores devours! I thought it was some kind of kinky French thing for an embarrassingly long time and never put it together with snack food for a party, which clearly should be spelled o-r-d-e-r-v-e-s. Do you know at one point I thought about a food truck that only served finger food? I'd call it Orderves spelled like it sounds and they'd be really super fancy and served on square plates with sauce drizzles but made out of, like hot dogs and Jell-O. Oh, it's dark in here."

The kitchen was all reflective angles and racing shadows in the light of Frank's phone.

"Let's pack a picnic lunch and go back to the ballroom," Frank suggested. It wasn't exactly light there, but it was better than this.

"You're full of brilliant ideas," Anita said. "Got a basket?"

They couldn't find a basket, and it was challenging but kind of fun ransacking the cabinets with Anita firmly attached to his side. They did find a serving tray, and a few bags of high-end croutons.

"As kitchens go, I'm kind of underwhelmed," Anita said. "I couldn't cook anything here! There are no spices, no flour, no sugar, no talking mice or singing crabs!"

"It's a rental," Frank said apologetically. "I guess you're supposed to bring your own talking mice and singing crabs."

"I'd kill for a bag of chips," Anita said with a sigh, peeking over Frank's shoulder into a cabinet. "But I guess croutons will do. What's in the fridge?"

This, at least, was a treasure trove, and they heaped the tray with artful swirls of cheese and cold cuts and tiny foods that Frank couldn't even identify.

"What's this one?" Anita asked, holding up semi-transparent globes on toothpicks with pink plastic flamingos on the end.

"They look kind of like pickled pearl onions?" Frank guessed.

There were skewers with fruit interspersed with white cheese, drizzled in some kind of dark sauce and sprinkled with something green.

"What's on this?" Anita asked raptly.

"I have no idea."

"How can you not know what you're serving at your own party?" Anita asked.

"I have people!" Frank protested. "They handle stuff!"

"I had no idea you could put so many *things* on toothpicks," Anita said as they loaded their serving tray with a few of everything that looked good. "Oh, that looks like it's wrapped in bacon, grab me three of those. And some of those tiny shrimp! We'll need something to drink!"

"Wine…" Frank started, and he finished in chorus with Anita, "Probably too penthouse," and they both burst out laughing. He found a few bottles of water.

"Glass bottled water," Anita said skeptically. "That *is* fancy. But I suppose it's better for the environment? I try to be mindful of that, but I have to admit I have one of those K-cup machines at home for coffee."

She took one of the boxes of cupcakes with them as they hurried back to the ballroom with Frank carrying their loaded tray. Anita glanced behind them frequently. "Did you hear something?" she asked. "I felt a cold draft."

Their own sounds were all that Frank could hear in the weirdly silent building. "Bloody hooks?" he asked, and while he loved that Anita squeaked and pressed even closer up against him, it nearly made him drop the heavy tray of food. "Whoops! It's probably just the building creaking as it gets cold."

"Are we going to freeze to death in here?" she wanted to know morbidly. Then she brightened. "Oh, but that will keep the food from going bad, at least!"

Frank wondered if suggesting that they could huddle together for warmth was going too far in a penthouse direction, and then they were stepping out into the relative brightness of the ballroom and he was looking for a table to put his tray down on.

Beside him, Anita gave a tiny shriek of fear and dropped her cupcake box.

CHAPTER 5

*A*nita didn't want to be a complete scaredy-cat in front of the nice, rich man who was so tolerant about being mistaken for a janitor and then pretending that the event was still on, just to humor her. He put up with her cuddling up to him for comfort in the terrifying dark in far too familiar a manner, but didn't for a moment act like that meant he could take liberties. Anita wasn't sure if she'd really mind liberties from him, and even suspected a few times that he might want to take them, the way he smiled sideways at her.

She'd always thought that *dancing eyes* was some kind of outrageous flowery description, but Frank's golden-brown eyes really did look like he was poised on the brink of laughter, or breaking into a foxtrot.

She was letting herself think about those eyes, trying to remind herself that being trapped by a storm in a giant empty building with no power was not at all frightening and probably there was *not* a serial killer locked in here with them in the dark and ghosts weren't real and...

They stepped into the ballroom, which was at first a

great relief because what light there was outside in the storm was filtering in through the tall windows, and then Anita's heart seemed to stop.

She wasn't aware that she'd screamed and dropped the cupcake box until it hit the floor, moments after Frank's heavily loaded tray crashed to the table where he'd poured her fanciful champagne.

"What is it?" he asked, snatching up one of the heavy bottles of water like a club and turning with impressive spryness.

And then he saw it, too.

When they'd left the ballroom, the great mechanical flamingo had come to a rest, and they had never gotten around to uncovering the smaller, commercial version.

Now both of them were uncovered, and both of them were moving as if they had each just been wound.

Frank looked around in alarm. "Hello?" he called into the shadows, brandishing his bottle. "Who's there?"

Only silence answered as they both held their breath and listened.

Even empty buildings usually had a background of sounds. There were always pipes creaking, fans whirring, distant HVAC systems, the hum of lights. Anita strained so hard to hear that she felt herself getting dizzy, and all she could make out was the constant batter of snow being blown against the windows, the creak of the slowing kinetic sculptures, and the pounding of her own heart. Her stomach added an embarrassing groan that was loud in the room.

"Sorry, that was me," she whispered.

Both of the flamingos ponderously came to a stop again, and no sound replaced their creaking.

"Did you rent a *haunted* event hall?" Anita hissed. "Or

did you build a giant enchanted flamingo that can start itself?"

Frank chuckled dryly and put the bottle down. "I didn't think I'd done either of those things." He picked the bottle right back up, then marched across the room to the sculptures.

Anita had never seen anything so brave or stupid. She gave a squeak of dismay at being left behind and scrambled after him, nearly tripping over her abandoned cupcake box. Frank put a hand out to her, and she gratefully took it, twining her fingers easily into his as she caught up.

"Maybe Tobias attached some kind of mechanism to make the unveiling more dramatic," Frank hypothesized. He put the bottle down and got his phone in his other hand again, moving the light over the sculpture and frowning in concentration.

"How'd the other one get uncovered?" Anita wanted to know.

Frank shrugged. "Maybe the covering jiggled off when the mechanism was activated? I'm going to bill my heart attack to that jerk, if that's what happened. He could have warned me." He had opened up a panel in the flamingo's breast and was eyeing the gears and cables inside the cavity. Finally, he snapped it closed again. "Well, whatever it is, I don't think it will happen again. Let's have some food to settle our nerves."

Anita wondered if he was trying to distract her, and realized that he hadn't confirmed that there was some kind of *mechanism*, but she didn't have a more reasonable explanation for what had happened, and her stomach was starting to make a whole host of embarrassing noises in the quiet room. "Food sounds great," she agreed plaintively. "Let's make a fort and put our backs up against a wall."

Frank, to Anita's surprise, took her idea for a fort quite literally and tipped over a few of the tables to make a barricade around a blank spot of wall that faced the stage. Anita rescued the cupcakes and brought the tray into their cozy new corner as Frank ransacked a supply closet and found a whole armful of drapes and table cloths. "You look cold," he offered.

Anita wasn't sure if she was cold, if all of her nerves were shot, or if her blood sugar had just reached new record lows, but she was actually shaking. She wrapped a royal blue semi-velvet drape around her like an emperor's robe and padded a place for them to sit on the floor with the rest of Frank's cloth. They could just see the flamingos over the comforting protection of the table, and the eerie statues didn't move once while they fell upon the contents of the tray.

It was easy to be distracted. Not only was Anita starving, the food was absolutely amazing, and Frank himself was more and more interesting to watch as the hunger in her belly was slowly sated. She had never realized how sexy someone eating things off a stick could be.

"I would never in my life have paired some of these things," she said, teasing a ball of cheese from her skewer with her teeth. "Dates and bacon should never be served separately again. And I am glad we're eating here instead of in the kitchen, because I probably actually would try to eat two thousand people's worth of these hors d'oeuvres and you wouldn't be able to fit me back out the door when the snow finally stops and we can leave."

"There's the big sliding cargo door at the loading dock," Frank said, doing something with his tongue to get his food off his toothpick that made the breath catch in Anita's throat. "I'm going to need it to leave myself because I cannot stop eating the tiny food on twigs. Have you tried the pearl onions?" He held one out.

It was perfectly natural to lean forward and eat one off the toothpick that he offered. Anita didn't realize until her lips closed around it that a) this brought her incredibly close to him, b) she probably could have just taken the toothpick with her hand, and c) that he smelled *fantastic*.

He was watching her avidly, like he wanted to eat *her*.

Then he turned pink and looked abashed, realizing that he was staring at her.

Anita managed to stab herself in the mouth with the toothpick as she turned the moment into something completely graceless. "Ow," she said around her pearl onion once she was at a safe distance.

"I'm so sorry," Frank said, looking like a dog that had just been snacking from a plate of cookies.

Anita wasn't sure what he was apologizing for. She wasn't sure *he* was sure what he was apologizing for. She ought to say something, but she couldn't figure out what that was supposed to be until the moment had gotten weird and she decided to say nothing.

He opened one of the bottles of water for her, and Anita took a long, grateful swig.

This, unfortunately, illuminated a new problem that Anita was having.

"Are you okay?" Frank asked after a few moments while Anita cursed her tiny bladder and the cups of coffee she'd drunk to stay awake all night frosting cupcakes.

She gave a noisy sigh. "I have to pee," she said plaintively.

CHAPTER 6

$\mathscr{F}$rank made a sound that probably betrayed that he was trying to decide whether to cough politely or laugh and didn't quite manage either. It was very un-gazillionaire of him. "Let's go find the ladies' room," he offered gallantly. "I think it's on the second floor."

Anita unwrapped herself from the velveteen drape and stood up. "I'm really sorry," she said, looking embarrassed.

"Bodies," Frank said with a shrug. "They always want inconvenient things, like food and sleep." *And sex,* his flamingo added hopefully.

That's not helping anything, he replied with gritted teeth.

He offered her his hand to help her over the sideways table and was delighted when she accepted it. He was even more delighted when she left it there as he led her to the back of the event hall where the stairs went up to the second level.

"I think it's back this way," he said when they got to the top of the stairs, hand-in-hand.

It got darker as they went further down the hallway,

and Anita drew closer and closer to him as they walked. He had to pull out his phone again to use the light and find the doors to the bathroom, two of them together with fancy silhouettes for his and hers.

They stopped before the ladies' room and Anita gave a little squeak as she seemed to realize that Frank wasn't going to go in with her. "You can take my phone." He held it out to her.

She reluctantly let go of his hand and took the phone. "Thanks," she said quietly.

"Are you reconsidering?"

"I am," she confessed, fidgeting in place. "My bladder is not."

She raised her chin in an impressive show of bravery and opened the door, letting the beam of light swing over the bank of sinks and stall doors. "Here I go," she said. "In by myself."

"There you go," Frank agreed.

"Really, I'm going in," Anita insisted without moving.

"I know you can," Frank encouraged.

"I am ridiculous," Anita said, and she finally marched in and let the door swing closed behind her.

Frank wondered at how bereft he felt when the door latched between them.

He'd known this woman a few scant hours and already, he could not imagine his life without her unquenchable sunshine.

It was also very quiet without her chatter, and Frank was aware of the vast emptiness of the building around them.

All the hair at the back of his neck suddenly rose. At first, Frank was confused by his warning instinct, thinking that it was just that his mate was out of his sight for the first time since they'd met and his flamingo was being protective. Then he realized that he was hearing footsteps.

Someone else *was* in here with them.

He didn't want to frighten the already high-strung Anita, so he hadn't admitted that he still didn't have any idea why the sculptures had been in motion when they returned to the ballroom. There didn't appear to be any sign of tampering and his off-the-cuff theory that there was some kind of last-minute automation had proved at a glance to be wrong.

But the conjecture had been comforting to Anita and Frank had decided that it was better to let her continue to believe it than squash it before he had a better idea of what had actually happened.

The footsteps seemed to be coming towards him from around a corner down the dark hallway and Frank reached for his phone, wondering if it was pointless to call the police in the middle of a snowstorm that had already taken out the power and probably closed every major road for miles. Then he remembered that Anita had his phone anyway, just as there was suddenly a shrill scream from the bathroom.

He slammed into the bathroom door before he remembered how door handles worked and it groaned at his impact, probably only frightening Anita further.

He fumbled for the latch and got it open, peering into the inky darkness of the bathroom. "Are you all right?" he called.

He had to blink for a moment to adjust his eyes and could finally pick out the silhouette of her head peeking from behind a stall door.

"Yes," she squeaked. "Your phone light turned off, and it scared me. That's all. Sorry."

Frank's whole body was sizzling with adrenaline, and

he could not quite keep himself from stepping further into the bathroom and sweeping Anita into his arms. It only occurred to him after she was there that she had stepped to meet him, and he wasn't sure who was trembling more.

"I didn't mean to frighten you," she mumbled into his collarbone, along with other words that Frank only partly heard, something about *ladies' room* and *washing hands*.

She belonged in his arms like this; she fit him perfectly, all soft curves and perfect height. He could cradle every part of her, lean his jaw into her hair. Frank's tremor swiftly became less about fear and more about need. She was warm against him and yielding in all the right places.

If she tipped her head up to meet him, he'd be able to kiss her…but she didn't and after a few moments, she gave a shuddering sigh and stepped back instead.

Frank's flamingo gave a keen of regret, but Frank let her go.

He only realized that certain parts had grown unmistakably hard when there was space between them again, and he wondered in chagrin if she'd noticed.

CHAPTER 7

*A*nita noticed Frank's hard-on.

It was hard *not* to notice.

Anita promptly rearranged the emphasis in her head.

It was *hard* not to notice.

And he felt even better all snuggled up in a comforting hug that he had when she was just casually clinging to him like a scared rabbit. He was so deliciously built, with seriously impressive muscles underneath his janitor-comfortable clothing. It was the strongest, sexiest hug that Anita had ever had.

Peeling herself out of that embrace took all of her crumbling self-control. "Sorry I scared you," she said sheepishly. "Your phone just ran out of juice and I guess I screamed. I mean, I seem to be screaming a lot. I didn't think of myself as a…uh…screamer, but here we are."

Now she'd said *scream* way too many times. She fished the dead phone out of her pocket and handed it to him, trying not to think too hard about how he might make her scream, or read too much into a kind hug that suggested he might actually be into her.

Because guys who were into her were always trouble.

It was fun and games when things were friendly and funny and flirty, and there was the brief thrill of feeling attractive instead of just goofy, but after that, it always got weird. *She* made it weird. And she didn't want it to be weird with Frank.

Besides the fact that he was really cute and fabulously rich, they were trapped together in a rapidly chilling event hall in the middle of the storm of a century, and there was nowhere to run if he turned out to be a serial killer.

And honestly, she really liked Frank and didn't want to ruin what she was actually starting to feel was a blooming friendship. He had a great sense of humor and he was sweet and willing to be silly with her. Anita felt comfortable and safe with him.

He was being really quiet now, so probably she'd already done the deed and gone from adorable and fun to be sequestered with to someone who screamed too much and had a bladder the size of a tomato. It was hard to make out his expression in the dark, spooky bathroom. It was hard to make out even the shape of him. There was a tiny frosted window up near the ceiling, but it let in almost no light.

"Sorry," she mumbled.

"For what?" he asked promptly.

"For screaming? For being terrified and terrible with people?" She probably should have kept the second thought to herself. Normal people kept those confessions on the inside.

"I'd have screamed too," Frank admitted. "All alone in a bathroom when the light went out."

Anita couldn't help but scoff, "You would not. You have probably never screamed in your life."

"I have," Frank insisted. "Like a *girl*." He swiftly added, "Not that there's anything wrong with girl screams."

He was so *nice*.

"I have to wash my hands," Anita said firmly. She fumbled her way to the sink and turned on a tap, rinsing her fingers longer than usual because she couldn't see if she'd gotten the bubbles off. It was ice cold and she splashed a little on her face, getting her shirt wet as she did. "I feel like an Antarctic explorer," she said. "In one of those research stations where they study penguins."

She couldn't remember where the towels were, so she dried her hands on her pants and turned back to the dark, looming form of Frank.

"Do you…like birds?" he asked unexpectedly.

Anita guessed it wasn't the oddest question he could have asked; she was the one who'd brought up penguins. "Sure," she said. "I mean, on a case-by-case basis. I have a neighbor with a parrot that bit me once when I was watching their house, but for the most part, yeah, I like birds."

"I have something I need to tell you," Frank said hesitantly.

Here it comes.

Anita felt her heart drop down into her toes. Was it going to be the familiar *I don't think of you that way* speech? The *I wouldn't mind doing it because we're trapped together and there's nobody better, but please don't assume it means anything* pitch? Frank seemed too kind to use the *I'm sorry for you so I'll sleep with you* line. And they'd already had the penthouse talk; only her cupcakes were for sale.

Also, she wasn't sure what any of that had to do with *birds.* Unless maybe he thought she didn't know about the birds and the bees?

Snick, snick, snick.

In the silence that stretched between them, the sound of footsteps in the hall was suddenly very loud, even though the person outside was clearly trying to sneak by. Anita knew from experience that sneaking in heels was very challenging.

Snick…

The sound stopped abruptly, right in front of the bathroom door, like they'd just realized that the conversation inside had quieted.

Anita stuffed her hand into her mouth to keep from screaming again. Frank took a swift step towards her and then turned so he could brandish his phone towards the door as he put an arm around her shoulders protectively.

They were definitely not alone in his haunted event hall.

Anita was shivering now, between the freezing water and her nerves. Why was someone here with them? Who was it? Her imagination, a runaway train at the best of times, was happy to supply the possibility of a serial killer, or an angry spirit, or a ferocious monster in high heels with a taste for baker's blood.

And nothing happened.

After a few moments, Frank left Anita's side and stalked bravely to the bathroom door, groped for the handle and flung it open…onto an empty hallway.

He peered out in each direction, and Anita crowded close behind him.

No one was there.

"I heard footsteps," she insisted. "I did."

"I did, too," Frank said. "And earlier, when you were in the bathroom alone."

Because *that* wasn't terrifying.

"The flamingo sculptures didn't start on their own, did they." Anita didn't say it like a question.

"I didn't want to frighten you," Frank said, with a grimace that she could see. It was brighter in the hall, and she could make out his features. It was always astonishing how handsome he was, even when he was looking sheepish.

Anita knew there were several ways that she could take that. He could be just a generally dishonest guy. He could be one of those guys who thought he knew what was best all the time and thought he was protecting her with omissions of fact.

"I really want to be honest with you," he said softly.

He might be the kind of guy who had trouble being honest when Anita was perfectly happy leaping to assumptions like 'you're a janitor,' and 'there's a logical reason for this really creepy thing.'

"It's usually the best policy," Anita said. She kept swiveling her head, looking to each end of the hallway suspiciously. It was eerily quiet again, not even the tiniest little *snick* of footsteps or any sounds other than their own conversation and breathing. She could barely even hear the storm anymore, this deep in the building.

When Frank slipped his hand into hers, it felt like the most natural thing in the world, and Anita let herself twine her fingers with his. It made sense to let her think there was a reason that the flamingos had been wound up. A reason that wasn't 'we're stuck in a building with a ghost or maybe a murderer.'

They headed back down the hallway towards the stairs that went down to the open ballroom below and Anita felt safer in the brighter and more familiar territory. Their table fort looked undisturbed from above, though they couldn't see the possibly haunted sculptures from here.

"What did you want to tell me?" she asked as they got to the top of the staircase. It was the kind of staircase that a princess might walk down to make a grand entrance. Anita was more focused on not tripping down it because she was wired to eleven and her exhaustion was rapidly catching up with her.

Frank stopped right at the top of the stairs, and then drew her back a short way. "I think I should show you." He said it shyly, like he was getting ready to demonstrate a magic trick that he wasn't really sure about.

He took his hand back, and while Anita was still feeling a little lost and uncertain without having it to cling to anymore, he suddenly sort of shivered in place and she was staring into the yellow eyes of a gigantic, prehistoric pink bird.

I'm not going to scream, I'm not going to scream, I'm not going to scream.

Anita was concentrating so hard on not screaming that she forgot they were standing at the top of the stairs and nearly fell down them taking a big step backward.

Frank transformed back to human and caught her by the waist before she could humiliate herself by toppling ungracefully down the steps, doing a super careful dance of *touching-but-not-bad-touching-saving-you-ack!*

"You're a shifter!" she exclaimed, taking both of his hands in hers. "You're a *flamingo*! That's why you asked about birds! Oh, you're a *shifter*!"

CHAPTER 8

Frank wasn't absolutely sure that Anita would have fallen down the stairs if he hadn't caught her and pulled her back, but he *was* absolutely sure that if he'd let go of her, she would have fallen shortly after, she was capering so carelessly.

His flamingo was triumphant. *She's dancing for us! Our flock!! Our mate! We please her!*

Frank managed to guide her away from the most dangerous area, laughing helplessly as she clung to both of his hands and bounced like a sugar-high toddler.

"You're a shifter," she squealed in absolute glee. Frank was not sure he had ever witnessed such happiness. "I've never met a shifter before. I mean, I think one of my neighbors is one, because I never saw him at the same time as his cat, but nobody who was out about it, you know? Except on television, like that crazy bendy guy with the talk show. He's, what, a leopard? A flamingo is so much cooler!"

Shifters were not exactly secret anymore. They had been when Frank was a baby, but the shifter equality laws had been in effect by the time he was walking and shifting. Shifters didn't have to disclose themselves, and most of them chose to go quietly about their lives to avoid discrimination; there were still circles of people who thought that shifters were unnatural or demonic. For the most part, though, there were enough shifters, in all walks of life and privilege, that it was as generally accepted as being a characteristic rather than a quality.

Frank had only a very small circle of close friends and artists who knew that he was a flamingo, and they were all shifters themselves, some of them quieter about the knowledge than others. Tobias was trying to pressure him to go public with it, in order to improve the general impression of shifters using his prestige.

Anita sobered suddenly. "Could there be another shifter in here with us? Like…a mouse shifter or something?"

"It's possible," Frank agreed. That would explain how they'd stayed out of their way this long, but it didn't really do much to illuminate why there was someone here at all, or what they wanted.

"You don't have some kind of—" Anita flapped her hand. "Sonar? Telepathy?"

Frank shook his head. "Sorry to disappoint," he said.

"You do *not* disappoint," Anita said quickly. Frank thought she blushed then, but it was hard to make out in the gloomy light.

He was still holding her hands. Should he risk a kiss? She'd been so happy that he was a shifter, and not the tiniest bit disappointed he wasn't some kind of massive, manly shifter like a bear or an elephant or something. Was she blushing in invitation?

"Should we try to find them?" Anita proposed. To

Frank's disappointment, she took her hands back at last and he missed his chance to draw her close and kiss her.

"Our only flashlight is dead," Frank pointed out. "I mean…we could?"

Anita looked nervously down the shadowed hall. "I think I'd rather go back to our fort," she confessed.

"You look cold," Frank agreed.

Snuggle, his flamingo suggested.

CHAPTER 9

The flamingo sculptures were not moving when they cautiously descended to the ballroom, and Anita drew in a deep breath of relief. "I was half-afraid they would have come entirely to life this time," she confessed. "We'd come out to find that they were stalking around wrecking up the place."

She mimed a stiff-armed, stiff-legged robot and Frank did something more zombie or dinosaur than robot until they were both laughing so hard that the empty ballroom rang with it. If there was someone lurking around in the darkness, they had to know by now that they weren't alone and that Frank and Anita weren't scared of them.

Well, not very scared.

Okay, maybe Frank wasn't scared. Anita was still on full five-alarm alert. Plunging into the darkness alone in an unfamiliar bathroom was probably the most terrifying thing that had ever happened to her.

"Are you still hungry?" Frank asked when they had arrived back at their table fort.

Most of the *hors d'oeuvres* had been *hors devoured,* and

Anita shook her head. She was full and, now that the jolt of adrenaline had eased, she really just wanted to sit down for a little while in the comfortable-looking pile of curtains and tablecloths.

Frank, true to his bird nature, vaulted into the fort and made her a proper nest, then extended a hand to help her scramble over.

She found the bottle of water and took a good swig as she settled down into the cozy little space and pulled a tablecloth around her. When Frank looked like he might hover uncomfortably or set up some kind of perimeter march, Anita patted the spot beside her. Finding out that he was a shifter had made her feel safer with him than ever. All her very favorite stories had featured shapeshifters, and although he'd been very alarming as a flamingo—nearly as tall as she was and with a beak like a battle axe—she felt like he'd do a very solid job protecting her in either form.

Even from murderous ghosts.

He settled gracefully at her side, not quite touching, and they both leaned back against the wall behind them.

The box of cupcakes had survived being dropped, suffering no more than a little frosting lost to the lid. Despite saying that she wasn't hungry, Anita opened it and took out one with pink frosting that matched her stained fingertips. She handed the box to Frank, who selected a blue one.

That prompted her to say, "Can I ask you something that might be a little personal?"

Frank shrugged as he peeled his cupcake wrapper off. "Anything." He took a bite then, and his look of rapture delighted Anita. "This is the best cupcake I've ever had," he said earnestly.

"You paid enough for it," Anita sniffed. "And I'm worth the cost." That seemed like a very penthouse thing to say. "I mean…ah…you've got one thousand and ninety-eight of them left, at least?"

Anita concentrated on eating her cupcake so she wouldn't watch Frank eat too avidly. He licked the blue frosting off his own fingers, and she remembered her question.

"So, I learned that flamingos get their pink coloring from a kind of algae that they—that *you* eat, and that in zoos if they don't get this—*you* don't get this—not that you'd be in a zoo—they go white. *You* go white. Do you eat special algae diet to keep you so handsome and pink?"

His cheeks certainly didn't need a special algae diet. Even in the gray snowstorm light from the big ballroom windows, they were flamingo pink. "I take a supplement," he confessed quietly.

"You don't have to say it like that," Anita told him in an identical whisper. "I take melatonin and magnesium."

"It's kind of vain of me," Frank told her, laughing but maintaining their stage whisper. "It doesn't do a single thing but keep me pink, but it just…doesn't feel right to be white."

"I don't think it's any worse than dyeing your hair," Anita assured him. "It's totally fine. You're totally fine." She reminded herself to shut up a sentence earlier. "I mean, you're a fine flamingo."

Frank glanced shyly sideways at her. "Thanks," he said sincerely.

"What's it like being a gazillionaire?" Anita asked wistfully.

She didn't think that it might be a rude question until Frank didn't answer right away. "I'm sorry, that's probably—"

"Oh, you're fine," Frank hastened to assure her. "It's just that I'm kind of a new gazillionaire, and it's mostly on paper." He looked around surreptitiously and whispered to Anita, "I hope I'm doing it right."

Anita had to scoot closer and pat him on the arm. "I'm sure you're doing great," she said comfortingly. He had a really great arm, and she didn't really want to stop patting it. "Everyone says you're a really nice person. Very generous."

"They have to say that," Frank scoffed. "I'm a gazillionaire. Who's going to say bad things about someone who might impulsively buy them a swimming pool and an antique car?"

"Not me," Anita said. "You've been very kind. And I'm not just saying that because you might buy me a swimming pool or an antique car."

Frank was warm. They were kind of leaning into each other now, and Frank had an arm around her.

"Do you want a swimming pool or a car?" he asked, and Anita was alarmed to think he might be serious.

"No," she said. And in a feat of stunning self-control, she did not say what immediately popped into her mind, which was, *I only want you.*

It was a ridiculous thing to want this guy.

Well, no, it wasn't ridiculous to want *him*. He was good-looking and possibly the sweetest man that Anita had ever met, not the slightest bit stuck up, despite being impossibly rich and also a shifter. He was funny and smart and built like a cover model for a dirty book, on top of being a famous artist who donated most of his money to charity.

It was just ridiculous to think that she wanted him to want her.

Anita wasn't sure when she slipped from consciousness, thinking about how impossible everything about this whole day had been.

CHAPTER 10

It didn't take more than a few moments for Anita to fall asleep, and Frank almost stopped breathing because he didn't want to accidentally jostle her and wake her up. At first, she was just leaning heavily against him, then her head was lolling against his shoulder.

She wasn't exactly light, but Frank didn't mind holding her at all, propping her up with one arm and letting her head nestle against his collarbone. Would it be too forward to kiss the top of her head? She had the softest-looking hair, with tiny little dark brown curls escaping her French braid like a halo. Surely it wouldn't be too bad to tuck a few of those locks behind her perfect little ear, and if that meant brushing his fingers over her velvety freckled cheeks...

Snuggle, his flamingo said, in perfect contentment.

For a long while, Frank was happy just to sit and hold his mate. Then his brain returned to the puzzle of the person in the hall with them.

He and Anita had not been quiet at all. If someone had been trapped in the building with them, why wouldn't they join forces? Frank was happy to have Anita to himself, but it indicated a certain amount of *not supposed to be here* on the part of their mysterious companion that put Frank on edge.

It was someone who could vanish silently.

It was someone strong enough to wind the great flamingo sculpture, so not a child, even supposing a child had gotten in.

Frank thought best when he was writing things out in notes and sketches. He patted his sweatshirt and found a pen and a Wilson Kinetic promo notebook in a deep pocket. Anita was occupying his right side, but he was fortunately left-handed and could balance the pad on his left knee and take some notes.

Stealthy, he wrote. *Shifter?*

Why would they wind the flamingos if they were trying to stay out of sight? Impulse? Curiosity? Maybe they just thought that Anita and Frank would be gone longer?

Was it someone he'd hired for the charity ball? A server who hadn't left in time and was embarrassed to admit it? Frank made more notes, with lots of question marks, then moved on to less plausible ideas, unwilling to eliminate any possibilities.

Ghost?

If it was, it wasn't obviously haunting them.

The wound-up flamingos were pretty alarming, but the interloper had clearly been trying to sneak past the bathroom, not terrify them further. Why would they tip-toe past at all when they could vanish so convincingly a moment later?

It was hard to concentrate on the puzzle, which seemed largely harmless now that there was no sign of their mysterious companion. The building was still and silent, except for the gray noise of the storm outside. The wind whistled and moaned and battered snow against the windows.

Anita was warm and solid against him, everything about her making Frank feel like everything in his life had just fallen beautifully into place.

Flock, his flamingo murmured.

She was everything he'd never known to miss. He thought his career had been fulfilling, that his success had been satisfying, but now that he'd met Anita, he understood what it meant to be complete.

He frowned, remembering her vehement penthouse protest. It was definitely still possible to scare her off.

Flock, his flamingo repeated.

He had to figure out how to properly court her. He had to convince her that she was his everything…and he had no idea how to do that.

He had never dated all that much, and he wasn't sure what it entailed. Dinner? Drinks? Dancing? If his phone still had power, he'd text Tobias to see if he had any advice. For a guy who was barely five foot and sported a beard like a lap rug, he had no trouble finding female companionship. If anyone could give him direction, Tobias could.

Dancing, his flamingo was sure, but Frank was already having trouble wrestling back his bird's occasionally overwhelming instincts. Maybe he should write her poetry, or sing under her window.

Probably, he shouldn't try singing.

But he had pen and paper at hand and great incentive not to move while his mate napped at his shoulder.

Frank carefully turned the page and started writing.

> *My flamingo thinks you're swell*
> *To tell the truth, I do as well.*

You came into my life with snow
You brought with you a happy glow.

I know you are my destiny,
Please say you will stay with me.

Frank looked at the words he'd written and groaned quietly. Singing was looking better and better.

He flipped the page back and frowned at the notes he'd made for their unwelcome visitor.

Then he frowned at his flamingo sculpture. Although he sometimes had trouble remembering it, his work was worth fabulous amounts of money. Could someone be skulking around with plans to *heist* it?

Frank wrote down *thief.*

Then he shook his head. There was no way that anyone could get away with a three-hundred pound mechanical sculpture in the middle of a snowstorm. It was possible that they could pry out a few of the larger gemstones, but the real value of his pieces lay in the clockwork mechanism and the grandness of scale. There was also no resale value in huge, distinctive, one-of-a-kind statues. Theft didn't really make sense.

He crossed off *thief.*

Then he flipped back to the poem and crossed over it with two big strokes.

He wasn't going to try to be something he wasn't. He was just going to *tell* Anita that she was his everything and promise to love her forever.

Flock, his flamingo said happily.

CHAPTER 11

*A*nita woke up drooling on a billionaire's shoulder and chagrin jerked her up out of his arms so fast that she knocked his chin with the top of her head.

"Ow, sorry, ow," she said. "I'm graceless."

"Hi, Graceless," Frank said with a smile. "Nice to meet you. I'm Frank." He was so gorgeous, and his mouth was so genuine. "I'm a janitor here at the Wild and Wet Charity Gala and Sleepover."

Who *wouldn't* have been able to smile back at that? Anita wondered, putting a hand to her head sheepishly. "Oh," she said then, because it finally occurred to her that she could see Frank really well now, and that was because sunlight was streaming in through the big bay windows.

The storm had broken, and from their vantage in the table fort, Anita could look up into the sky where big, puffy clouds were breaking apart like giant golden cupcakes.

"It's gorgeous," she said, and that was even before they both scrambled to their feet and could look out over the river and the valley far below. The landscape was covered in deep, fluffy drifts of snow, all silver and tinted in pastel blues. It was a painting, or a childhood memory, a perfect moment frozen in time.

"I wish I was an artist," Anita said wistfully. "I wish I had any hope of capturing this view, this moment, this…" she ran out of words and flapped a hand uselessly.

"It's beautiful," Frank said, but when she glanced over at him, he wasn't looking outside at all, only gazing at her, like she was the painting.

The power was still off, and the wind had stopped, too, so it was eerily quiet.

"How long was I asleep?" Anita asked, touching her hair self-consciously. She'd braided it the night before, so it was probably doing that thing where she looked sort of fuzzy all over. Frank's hair looked perfect. Her fingers were still pink, she realized, and that reminded her that Frank was a flamingo. She just kept herself from squealing.

"A few hours, I think. My phone is dead and I don't have a watch." He was rotating his arm like it was still asleep, and it probably was if Anita had been leaning all of her weight on his shoulder for a few hours.

"I'm so sorry," she said. Then she remembered something else. "Is there any sign of our creepy creeper person?"

"Not a peep," Frank said. "The only sound I heard was wind, and you snoring."

"I didn't!" Anita was mortified. "Tell me I didn't!"

Frank held up his fingers, close together. "A little?"

Mortified but laughing, Anita stretched and yawned. Maybe they had imagined the footsteps. Maybe the flamingo sculpture had…been some kind of mechanical fluke? The hall certainly felt a lot less haunted with brilliant sunlight streaming in.

"My foot's asleep," she said, wiggling her toes and

feeling the warning tingle that would come before the painful stage. "I bet the roads are all snowed in, too."

"It will be hours before they get the plows up here," Frank guessed. "Maybe not even until tomorrow. We're kind of off at the end of things here."

"Brrr," Anita said. "It's sunnier, but it's not a lot warmer." Frank had been more than just fun to cuddle up next to, he'd also been a great source of heat. Her foot was coming awake, and she stomped it to work the blood back into it.

Frank bounded back into their fort and found a table-cloth that he folded into a manageable cloak that he masterfully wrapped around her.

"I feel like an Irish princess," Anita said, swirling around in place. "'Come, Frank. Is the Wet and Wild Charity Gala still on or did I sleep through it?'"

"'Frank, the Irish janitor, at your service, m'lady,'" he said gallantly, with an utterly terrible Irish accent. "'You snored through the boring speeches and now the mingling is in full swing and I can hear the orchestra tuning up. Can I carry your train?'"

"'No, no,'" Anita insisted, gathering the dragging cloth and draping it over one arm. "'You are Frank the Janitor and you bow to no tablecloth and'…ow…my foot."

It was the sort of pain that made Anita giggle and gasp, not genuinely in agony, but so deeply uncomfortable that she couldn't ignore it and had to limp around with Frank hovering helplessly over her while she tried to force circulation back down to her toes.

"Okay, okay, it's better," she finally said, clutching at Frank's arm. "I'm such a dork. I bet real Irish princesses never let their feet go to sleep."

"I imagine that royalty has servants to follow them around and rub their extremities while they sleep," Frank said. He snapped his fingers. "I should have massaged your feet while you slept."

Anita figured he wasn't serious, but the idea of a guy like Frank rubbing her toes brought up a lot of those penthouse feelings that she'd been trying to ignore.

CHAPTER 12

Frank had loved having Anita snoring on his shoulder, even when half his body went numb from her weight and she drooled on him.

But he loved having her awake and so full of life that even a giant deserted ballroom didn't feel empty. She filled up the whole space with her energy and playfulness.

"We should do something," he proposed impulsively. "Play a game or something."

"Not a—"

"Not a penthouse game," Frank laughed. "Truth or Dare, or I Spy, or Simon Says."

"It's still kind of dark for I Spy," Anita observed. "And Truth or Dare seems risky with you. How do you play Simon Says with two people?"

"I, er, guess you just tell me what to do and I lose if you don't say Simon says and I do it?"

"Simon says stand on one leg, flamingo-man."

Frank obediently stood on one leg.

"Now put it down."

He caught himself just before doing it, and Anita gave him a golf clap.

"Simon says hop," she challenged.

Frank did, to his flamingo's delight. *We're dancing for her!*

It's a game, Frank tried to explain to the joyous bird. *We can only do what Simon says and we lose if we do what she says, but Simon doesn't.*

Frank's flamingo was not happy about the idea of losing.

"You're good at this," she said, after sending him through a series of increasingly complicated commands, failing to trick him into doing what Simon didn't say. She let him stop hopping, but she didn't say a word about putting his foot down.

Frank had to concentrate, still balanced on one leg while he patted his head and rubbed his stomach in a counter-clockwise direction. An idea suddenly occurred to him.

"Now change directions."

Frank might have failed the test on his own, but his flamingo was adamant. *She didn't say Simon says, we do **not** change directions.*

"We should make this interesting," Frank suggested, once he'd verified that his hand was not going to change directions without his conscious control.

"Strip Simon Says?" Anita asked innocently.

She said strip! his literal-minded flamingo shrieked. *Simon says!!*

It took every shred of Frank's concentration to continue rubbing his hand across his stomach and patting his head while still maintaining his balance on the one leg.

That's not what she meant, Frank said firmly. His flamingo pouted.

"I meant a bet," he said carefully. "If you can get me to

do something Simon doesn't say, you can have the flamingo statue."

"The flamingo statue worth a gazillion dollars?" Anita blinked at him in astonishment.

"Sure. It would be yours." Forming words while making his hands do opposite things and standing on one foot was the absolute limit of Frank's attention span.

"What would I do with it?" Anita wanted to know.

"You wanted to put it on your van."

"Not seriously," she protested. "I couldn't afford the insurance. Besides, it's supposed to be auctioned off for charity. I can't steal it from the orphans! Or the flamingos! Or the orphaned flamingos, or whatever!"

Frank's flamingo was a little miffed that she didn't want the giant statue of him.

"Fine," Frank compromised. "You can have one of the little yard-sized flamingos."

Anita considered. "Do I have to pay taxes on it?" she wanted to know. "I know that it can be complicated when you win sweepstakes."

"I'll have my accountant pay the taxes for you," Frank promised.

"What do you get if you win?" Anita said skeptically.

"A date," Frank said, squashing his flamingo's alternate ideas.

"A penthouse date?" Anita asked suspiciously.

"No, just a date," Frank said swiftly. "I'll take you out to a swanky restaurant, your choice, and we can go dancing if you want…"

He nearly lost the bet at that exact moment as his flamingo all but exploded into feathers of glee.

Dancing!!

CHAPTER 13

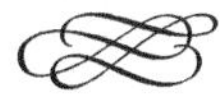

*A*nita was impressed.

Frank would have been pretty awe-inspiring under most circumstances, but here he was, being funny and coming up with good ideas while she was making him stand on one foot doing crazy things with his arms. And he was playing for a date? That was pretty flattering.

The pile of fabric in their fort was looking pretty tempting, actually, and Anita had a hot moment wondering how far she could get Frank to go with Simon Says. Would he take off his sweatshirt and shirt so she could see if his chest was as gorgeous as she imagined it was? Would he kiss her if she told him to? Or lay her down and make sweet love to her?

It would probably be hard to do on one leg.

Frank was gorgeous—and a shifter!—and he was so nice that Anita wanted to trust him and let herself feel all those bedroom feelings.

But she didn't dare.

She was running out of things to challenge him with

and it occurred to her that it was probably as bright in the building as it was going to get.

"Do you want to go exploring?" she asked, trying not to stare at Frank too obviously. "It's light right now. Maybe we should look for our ghost before it gets dark and raid the kitchen before everything goes bad."

"An excellent plan," Frank agreed cheerfully.

Anita half-expected him to stride out, forgetting about her stand on one leg command and she held her breath in anticipation.

But he was still patting his head and rubbing his stomach as he turned and hopped towards the back hallway.

"You can stop rubbing your stomach," Anita told him as she caught up with him, wondering how on earth he was managing to keep his limbs all synched up.

He gave her a cheeky smile and continued with his jerky hop-rub-pat.

"Simon says you can stop rubbing your stomach," Anita corrected.

He did, with a sigh of relief, and they continued on.

They made it out to the front entrance, and Anita gaped around. It was not well lit, but there were enough windows letting in light to see the marble floor and the fancy art. There were sculptures in alcoves all around the big lobby area, and everything was velvet and gold, like pictures she'd seen of old opera houses.

"If we're explorers, we should be thorough," Frank said, marching one-legged to the first door on the right. It was locked. "Probably a supply closet?" he guessed.

"You're the janitor," Anita pointed out. "You should know!"

The next door opened onto a coat check room, and there was one lone coat hanging there, a ticket on its sleeve suggesting someone had mistakenly left there it long ago. Frank offered it to Anita, but she demurred in favor of her Irish princess cloak. There was a broom in the corner, and Frank hefted it thoughtfully, then brought it with them.

If he'd been heroic with a bottle of water, that was nothing compared to Frank wielding a broom like a sword. On one leg.

The following door was a large storage room, and it was full of folding chairs and tables and spooky dark corners. Frank hopped bravely in, hollered, "Show yourself, ghost!" and then tripped over a low dolly he hadn't seen in the dark.

They left that room laughing and clinging to each other. Anita didn't penalize him for putting his leg down to save his balance.

CHAPTER 14

*A*lthough it was brighter than it had been, not all the rooms had windows, and as they left the lobby and the ballroom behind, the halls got darker and Anita found herself closer and closer to Frank.

That wasn't such a bad thing. He leaned on her a little as he hopped along.

"It's often rented as a conference center," Frank explained. "These are all the meeting rooms back here, and they have walls between them that can pull back and forth for bigger and smaller classes. I've attended a few trade shows here. Truly yawn-worthy stuff, with panels like *Accounting tips for wholesale import of small titanium screws from Elbonia* and *Obscure regulations for selling depictions of fowl in the state of Kentucky.*"

They peered into a few of them, letting their eyes adjust to the darkness, but there were no sounds or signs of people, just echoing empty rooms with industrial carpet and low popcorn panel ceilings.

Frank gave his challenge to each empty space, brandishing his broom. "Show yourself, ghost!"

No one showed themselves. There were no sounds of footsteps that weren't theirs.

They wandered quickly to the end of that long hall and found that it stopped in a T-intersection. "That's the way to the kitchen and the back entrance of the ballroom," Frank said, and he turned the other way. There was a meeting room to their right, with a dozen doors along the hallway opening into it and all the interior wall panels folded away so that it was one giant space instead of half a dozen little ones.

To their left, as they walked, was a bank of windows. They were on the not-sunny side of the building, and deep drifts of snow obscured the window, but there was enough light that it was all just a little eerie, not truly frightening.

It helped to have Frank at her side, and sometimes, when he wasn't imitating a one-legged sand creature from Star Wars with his broom, they were holding hands.

Not romantically, Anita told herself. It was just…convenient. Friendly. It wasn't a *penthouse* thing. It was just that she was helping him balance, because she was really starting to wonder if he was going to stay on one leg forever if she didn't release him. Did he really want a date with her that badly?

"I wanted to ask you something!" Anita remembered, as they got to the end of that hall, which bent around to return to the lobby.

"Anything," Frank said promptly.

"This charity event was to preserve wetlands for wildlife," Anita said. "Are those…like wild family members? Do you have a flamingo wife and kids down in Florida or something?"

Frank burst out laughing even as Anita recognized how absurd the question was.

"No," he assured her. "As far as I know, the flamingos

down there are only flamingos, not shifter flamingos. Tobias is the one who picked the charity, because I'd already done the sculpture, and he has a weird sense of humor."

"Tobias is your friend?" Anita said wistfully. She didn't have many friends left since she'd moved.

"My very best friend," Frank said without a moment of hesitation. "He runs Wilson Kinetic because I'm hopeless at it and he was the one who said it would work."

"Does he know what you are?"

"Yes," Frank said. "But I don't know what he is. He jokes that he's a gnome, but no one believes him."

"Like…a garden gnome?"

Frank shrugged. "So he says. And who am I to judge? I turn into a giant pink bird. I have to figure it's *gnome* big deal."

Anita felt her mouth quirk into a smile. "Gnome sweet gnome."

"There's no business like gnome business," Frank countered.

"I'll be gnome for Christmas!" Anita sang, badly.

Frank replied with, "Country road, take me gnome!"

They were back at the lobby now, having walked the full circle of the convention rooms loop.

Frank took her hand and drew to a stop in front of her, his face sobering.

"Anita, it's kind of on that topic. That is, I want to be perfectly frank with you…"

Frank's sudden seriousness made Anita nervous. "Are you being Frank? Cause Anita moment." She paused, not sure if the joke had rung true. "Get it? Anita? You're Frank and…I need a moment…"

He laughed more like a loon than a flamingo, a hooting, honking, helpless laugh that had tears rolling out of his eyes as he clutched her and shook with humor.

"It wasn't that funny," Anita said, giggling along anyway because maybe it was. It was nice having someone who *got* her stupid sense of humor. It was also kind of nice being held up close to him in the throes of his amusement, even with the broom against her back. He was really *well-built* for a gazillionaire.

"You really are perfect for me," Frank said, wiping at his eyes. His gaze gained intensity. "I cannot imagine anyone I could love more. You're my destiny."

"Woah, woah," Anita said, freezing in his arms. "I mean, this has been fun, and you're really cute for a janitor, but we had the penthouse talk, and oh—" She stared back at him. "That *mates* thing. It isn't just a crazy story?"

There were a lot of rumors about shifters, and Anita wasn't clear on what was real and what was sheer speculation. Some people insisted that they were mutants with superpowers, some that they were aliens from outer space, or their descendants. She'd seen claims that they all had X-ray vision and incredible strength, that they were all secretly cannibals, or farming people for food, or that they had mind-control powers, or that they were part of a conspiracy to take over the government. The talk show shifter had certainly had some freaky flexibility.

But one of the more pervasive and considerably less believable stories was that every shifter had a fated mate, one true love that they recognized on sight. It was a beautiful fairy tale, and in Anita's opinion, entirely too good to be true.

But Frank was nodding slowly, and his grin had taken on a dreamy, besotted cast. He looked like he wanted to kiss her, and as much as Anita wanted him to do that, the whole idea of it terrified her.

She'd already tried being someone's *destiny* and that had been just *awful.*

"Oh, no," Anita said, carefully pulling herself out of his grasp. "No, no, no, no."

"No?"

"It's a one-syllable word for not a chance, mister."

CHAPTER 15

Frank had to stare. Even his flamingo, for once, was struck dumb. This wasn't how mates were supposed to work.

He was supposed to tell her that she was the one, perhaps in interpretive dance, and then...

Snuggle? his flamingo said hopefully.

Anita, however, was clearly not interested in snuggles and she stood apart from him with her arms crossed over her breasts. "Look, you seem really nice," she said, in that way that some people said babies were cute when they actually looked like squashed hams.

"But I don't believe in true love, and I'm not looking for a relationship, and I am especially not interested in being some kind of shifter trophy. I know you're a gazillionaire, and we're stuck together in the middle of a snowstorm, and that probably seems really romantic, but I'm not the kind of girl who swoons over a guy and please don't turn out to be some kind of creepy stalker who isn't going to be able to take no for an answer. Especially while we're trapped in your haunted event hall."

Frank was not going to be that kind of creepy stalker. That was the last thing he wanted to be. "I can take no for an answer," he said gruffly.

"You won't call and call and call and text me and then text my parents and lean on all my friends when I don't want to date you anymore and start hanging around my work and look for rentals in my apartment building and leave notes about how pretty I looked when I was jogging and stalking all my social media until I couldn't post anything publicly or get my mail without putting on a sweatshirt?"

Frank was outraged. "Wait, someone did that to you?"

Anita sat down on one of the tables by the front door and drew her legs up so she was cross-legged, everything about her posture looking uncomfortable. "Sort of. I mean, they said it was my fault because I was nice, because I wasn't good at saying no, and I'm better at that now, and the answer is no. That's why I'm not nice to people now, too."

"Who said that?" Frank wanted to know. "Who said it was *your* fault?" His flamingo honked in fury.

"My parents," Anita said mournfully. "My friends. The *police.*"

"They failed you," Frank snarled, and for a moment, Anita looked genuinely afraid. Frank had to remind himself that she was a young woman trapped alone in a powerless, possibly haunted building with a complete stranger. "And you seem really nice to me," he added more gently.

"It was a business thing," Anita protested. "I'm allowed to be nice for money. And I don't mean that in a penthouse way." She buried her face into her hands. "I'm so bad at people."

"You aren't bad at people," Frank countered. "People

were bad at *you*. You should be able to be nice to people without turning them into crazy stalkers. I *want* you to be nice."

Anita peeked through her fingers. "Everyone says I'm too nice," she said. "I've got no sense of boundaries. Too forward, too much, I mean listen to how much I'm over-sharing right this very moment. I'm sort of proving the exact point here."

"Is that why you moved here from California?" Frank asked quietly.

Anita nodded. "I figured he wouldn't follow me across the country. I mean, I'm a catch, but not a *moving expenses* catch. And I could make new friends that weren't *his* friends. I hoped."

Frank wanted to tell her she was utterly irresistible and that he'd certainly follow her across the country in a red hot minute, but he realized it was in bad taste considering what she'd been through.

Snuggle, his flamingo said mournfully. *Flock*.

Frank didn't have the slightest doubt that Anita was meant for him. Whatever else his annoying flamingo was good for, he trusted the bird's instincts and could not disbelieve that she was absolutely the most perfect mate in the world.

He also knew that if he pushed her too far, he'd lose her forever, and the last thing he wanted to do was scare her or have her put him in the same box as her previous pushy would-be beau.

She had wilted and was as expressively morose as she'd been irrepressibly full of joy just moments before. She was a tempest in a teacup, Frank thought. So much heart and personality in such a perfect package. He was angry at the idea of someone frightening her and making her feel like she had to dampen even a tiny bit of her beautiful spirit.

Then he glanced behind her, to one of the little alcoves with a statue in it.

If the power had been on, it would have been the focus of a spotlight, but with the power off, it was dramatically shadowed, each of the pieces of art barely discernible. Most of them were stone figures, vaguely Grecian, and some had animals.

So Frank had to stare at this one for a moment to realize that what had caught his eye was the barest glint in the shadowed recess. The reflection of an eye.

While he watched it, ostensibly trying to look as if he was only gazing at Anita, the shape resolved into a pale bird, exactly the shade of the stone figure holding a vase that it was perched on top of. It was an owl and its shining eye was completely unblinking.

Frank gripped his broom tighter.

An owl could fly silently. It might have even passed over their heads in the hallway, causing a brief, icy draft. A shifter, undoubtedly, and one with some kind of ill intentions, or they wouldn't be skulking around this way pretending to be pseudo-Greek stone.

"Look, you don't have to feel sorry for me," Anita said, probably assuming the worst from Frank's sudden silence. "I'm a big girl with big girl pants on, and I don't mean that in a *fat* way even if I am. I've made a new life for myself and I got this great gig for a charity event that might have gotten me out of debt if I could use it to reach some big new clients, and even though it's canceled, maybe I'll still be able to make it because——"

Whatever she was going to say next was cut off with a scream because the owl that Frank was keeping tabs on had finally blinked and confirmed that it was alive.

He charged forward with his broom and a war cry.

CHAPTER 16

*A*nita thought for one horrible moment that she'd completely misjudged Frank, the way she completely misjudged everyone, and she really had been trapped in an event hall with a serial killer—but it was *him*.

He came charging at her with a furious cry and Anita screamed, confirming that she was much more of a screamer than she'd ever guessed, and not in a good, sexy way.

She should never have been friendly with him, she thought, as Frank raised his broom. Or maybe she shouldn't have refused him. Maybe she should have just gone along with his crazy *mate* delusions until the power came back up and she could find a phone and call the police.

If the police even believed her.

As she winced and closed her eyes in anticipation of Frank's blow—morbidly wondering if it could hurt worse than her disappointment—he sprang to the top of the table she was sitting on and speared the sculpture behind her with his broom handle. Anita fell to the side in astonishment as a bird rose out of the alcove with a haunting hoot.

It was quickly out of Frank's range with the broom, circling the high ceiling around the chandelier, and Anita thought that would be the end of it.

She'd forgotten that Frank was a flamingo.

Or maybe she'd forgotten that flamingos could fly.

She definitely forgot to be afraid for herself as Frank launched himself into the air after the bird and spread giant pink wings.

The other bird was an owl, Anita realized, watching them circle each other, a white and black-barred snowy owl. It was far more maneuverable than Frank was, and a little smaller, but Frank was surprisingly agile for a waterbird, and he was holding his own whenever they met midair.

Honestly, as alarming and horrifying as it was to watch, Anita could not help but overlay the action with a comic musical soundtrack in her mind. The two of them smashed into the walls and lights, sending the chandelier into tinkling song, and they flapped their wings at each other and turned dizzying somersaults as they fought. Neither of them seemed invested in truly hurting each other, but Frank wanted to catch the owl and the owl didn't particularly seem to want that.

Frank honked, and the owl screeched until the lobby echoed with their cries and Anita had to stand up on the table and cheer him on, the tablecloth that had been wrapped around her slipping off as she jumped up. She grabbed it as it tried to slither away, just as the two fighting birds swooped alarmingly close. She flung the billowing cloth at them desperately, not entirely sure if she was trying to protect herself or insert herself into their battle.

It was a lucky shot, and the fabric swirled out over both

of them as if she was some kind of graceful Amazon and not just a plump baker with dye-stained fingertips.

They fell together onto the floor in a tangle of tablecloth and squirming lumps of bird and wing. Anita wasn't sure which was which when it landed, so she simply flung herself over both of them with her arms spread, hoping to stop the fight and capture the owl.

"Ow, ow, ow!" It was a woman's voice, and a woman's form underneath her now, and Anita rolled to pin her down as Frank shifted and wrestled his way out from underneath the other side of the tablecloth.

"Mercy!" the woman cried. "Ow, your *elbows!*"

Anita immediately felt terrible, never mind that the owl shifter had been haunting the hall and scaring the bejeebus out of them and possibly plotting their grisly deaths. She rolled away just as Frank grabbed the broom and got to his feet. They flanked the draped woman and Anita reached forward to pull the tablecloth away, feeling like a frumpy Vanna White.

The prize behind sheet number one is…

"Harriet Slade?!"

Her arch-nemesis was dressed in a slinky silver dress and matching heels, and her bright red hair looked considerably worse for the wear.

She sat up slowly, eyeing the business end of Frank's broom warily and holding her shoulder.

"Hi, *Anita.*"

Anita felt like her head was doing a record screech sound. "Harriet Slade?" she said again, sitting back on her heels. "What are you doing here?"

"This is your cupcake rival?" Frank said in astonishment. He didn't offer to lower the broom. "What are you doing here?"

Harriet glared between them, then decided that Frank

wasn't going to immediately hit her, slowly getting to her feet with her hands spread. Anita scrambled up with considerably less grace.

"Answer the question," Frank growled, taking one threatening step towards her. "Why are you here?"

Anita watched Harriet weigh her options, glancing up at the ceiling and rubbing her sore shoulder. Finally, she heaved a sigh and glared at Anita. "I was here to sabotage your cupcakes."

"My cupcakes? *Sabotage*?"

Frank let the tip of the broom droop. "Why would you do that? She was up all night making those cupcakes!"

Anita was warmed by his defense.

"Because cupcakes are a cutthroat business," Harriet protested. "Because she just waltzed into town and stole the event contract and half my sales and everyone…likes her cupcakes more." She had her arms wrapped around herself and looked for all the world like a kicked puppy.

Anita reminded herself not to feel sorry for her. *Sabotage!* Her *arch-nemesis!* "What were you going to do?"

Harriet reached into her cleavage and Frank immediately drew his broom up. "Careful," he warned.

"It's not like I have room for a gun in this dress," Harriet said, slowly drawing out a small plastic bag filled with sparkling powder. "And if I was going to kill you, I'd have done it earlier, while you were snuggling in your little fort."

Anita blushed at the idea of Harriet spying on them. It was lucky that she hadn't done anything more risqué than drooling on Frank in her sleep.

"Wait, you were going to drug my cupcakes?" Anita's imagination suggested that it was crack or cocaine or maybe some kind of mind control powder. "Is it poison?"

Was arsenic white? She thought it was supposed to be odorless and colorless.

"No!" Harriet said in outrage. "It's vinegar powder. I was just going to ruin them."

Frank gave an angry growl and poked her in the shoulder with his broom. "How dare you?" he bristled. Anita wondered if he'd be so gallant for just anyone, or if it was because she was his mate. He seemed like a gallant kind of person, so probably she shouldn't take it as personally as she wanted to.

Harriet's look was flatly unimpressed, but she winced when he made contact. "Look, I had the best cupcake shops in the whole city until she showed up! I was going to lose my biggest clients! And anyway, that was before I heard the whole stupid sob story about how you had to move here because of a creepy stalker." She looked at Anita then, and her gaze was golden-brown and unblinking. "I'm sorry you had to go through that."

She held out the vinegar powder packet like a peace offering. After a moment, Anita put her hand out and accepted it.

Frank didn't seem as willing to forgive. "Why did you come when the event was canceled?" he asked suspiciously.

"I wasn't exactly on the guest list," Harriet sniffed. "So no one bothered to tell me that it was canceled. I strained my wing getting here just before the storm. My plan was to come early and hide until the party got started, then mingle with the guests."

"You wanted to watch them hate my cupcakes," Anita said, feeling a complicated amount of respect for Harriet.

"Yeah," Harriet said sheepishly. "I thought it would be hilarious. Sorry."

"It would have been hilarious," Anita agreed. "I can't say that I would have done the same thing, because I'm not a jerk, but I still bet it would have been amazing. All those celebrities spitting out their cupcakes into their napkins!"

"They'd probably dare each other to eat them," Harriet said enthusiastically. She lifted an imaginary cupcake to her mouth. "'I'm sure it isn't as bad as Victoria Henning's hair,'" she said in a perfectly snobby voice as she mimed taking a bite.

Frank looked between the two of them and finally let his broom rest on the floor again. "If you didn't want us to know you were here, why did you wind the flamingos?"

Harriet spread her hands as if it was perfectly obvious. "I didn't expect you to come back to the ballroom! There's a penthouse upstairs. I figured that you'd go straight up there after you hit the kitchen. Duh. And I'd never seen one of your fancy machines in motion and I didn't think I'd ever have the opportunity to again." She squinted at them. "Why *aren't* you up there?"

Frank was doing a bristly protective shuffle in place like he wanted to come and stand between them. "I don't want to make Anita do anything she doesn't want. I only bought her cupcakes."

"I wasn't asking you, you cotton candy goose," Harriet snarked.

Anita blinked. "Me? Well, you heard…"

Frank really did come and stand between them then. "She doesn't have to answer you."

"Don't get your feathers in a twist, hot legs," Harriet said. She craned her head to look around him at Anita. "I just want to point out that this guy is clearly not the jerk who chased you onto my turf. He's been a total gentleman with you. He's hot, you're into each other, what's the holdup? He even wrote you really awful poetry."

Frank gave a little jolt. "You saw that?"

"Owls have really good vision in dim light," Harriet

said as if it was really obvious. That seemed to be her default tone.

"You wrote me poetry?" Anita said to Frank's back.

"It's kind of terrible," Frank said, turning to look down at her. "Sorry. I'd already decided not to inflict it on you."

"I kind of want you to inflict it on me," Anita confessed.

"Oh my god, you two are disgusting. Just *neck* already."

CHAPTER 17

Frank was definitely happy to have an answer to the riddle of the haunted event hall, and he loved the idea that Harriet thought that he and Anita were 'into each other,' but he wasn't all that pleased with the rival baker's constantly condescending tone. His flamingo was outraged that she'd come here to ruin their mate's culinary reputation, though he was a fan of the necking idea.

"What are we going to do with you?" he asked generally.

"We could call the police," Anita suggested. "Except that your phone is out of power."

Frank looked thoughtfully at Harriet, who gave a bark of laughter and met his gaze with challenge. "I'm not going to give you my phone so that you can call the cops on me. Besides, I haven't actually done anything wrong. You're the one who assaulted *me* with a broom."

"You're trespassing," Frank pointed out. "You didn't have an invitation."

"Oh help, I got lost in the snowstorm of the century! I needed shelter! All I tried to do was stay out of your way!"

Harriet's innocent act wasn't terribly convincing. "Look, I didn't hurt anyone, and I didn't take anything, and you've still got two thousand unmolested cupcakes, for all the good they'll do you. I didn't *have* to tell you what I was planning to do, that was a gesture of good faith. And I decided not to do it anyway."

"I don't want her to get in trouble," Anita said, because she had a heart seven times the size of the flamingo statue.

"I thought you said that cupcakes were a cutthroat business," Frank said, mystified.

"A whole lot of Westerns would have been much shorter movies if they'd just built a town big enough for the two of them," Anita laughed. She extended a hand to Harriet. "Look, I hope there are no hard feelings. I didn't mean to encroach on your territory. Maybe we can work out…like a customer custody schedule or something."

"I feel bad for planning to destroy your cupcakes and crush you like a bug," Harriet said just as frankly, taking Anita's hand and giving it a sharp shake. "I've been wanting to specialize in fancy wedding cake decorating more anyway. I'll send you my extra cupcake business." She made it sound like a careless concession.

"And I'll send you my extra wedding cakes," Anita said kindly.

"Just weddings?" Harriet asked shrewdly.

"I'm not going to give up the rest of the holiday cakes for a few measly cupcake orders," Anita protested.

Even as Frank admired Anita's keen business sense, Harriet burst out laughing. "You're alright, sugar queen."

"You're not half bad for a baker baron," Anita retorted.

"Maybe…we can be friends?"

Frank didn't trust Harriet for a hot moment, but Anita bounded forward and impulsively hugged her.

"Oh, sorry," she said, when Harriet patted her awkwardly and squirmed away.

"You weren't kidding about being bad with boundaries," Harriet said.

Frank rather liked that about Anita, and he thought that Harriet looked a little like she did, too, sort of embarrassed and delighted and disgusted all at once.

"It's been kind of a long, weird day," Anita said frankly. "And I'm a hugger."

Harriet met Frank's eyes over Anita's head. "Enjoy *that*, super pink."

Frank wasn't sure what to say to that. "Thanks? I will?"

"Well, this has been real," Harriet said, brushing off the skirt of her sparkly silver dress. "It looks like the storm has cleared up enough for me to get home, strained wing or not and as fun as this has all been, I am going to jet before I die of sugar poisoning."

Not really sure what else to do, Frank walked her to the front doors and courteously opened them for her. A great deal of snow had drifted up against them, and it took Frank his full weight on the door to get it open.

"Miss me!" Harriet called, shifting back into an owl and bypassing the hip-deep snowbank by lifting up into the air. She flew somewhat raggedly, but was gone by the time Frank had wrestled the door shut again.

Then he really was alone in the deserted event hall with only Anita.

All he had to do now was win Simon Says and get his date with her so that he could sweep her off her feet.

Dancing! his flamingo said hopefully.

CHAPTER 18

"Well, that's the mystery solved," Anita said. "I feel like Scooby Doo. Velma of course. The short, nerdy one." She looked sideways at Frank. "You're Fred, of course, all handsome and rich."

"If it weren't for us meddling kids," Frank said knowingly. "I guess this means we're back to Simon Says." He made a show of stretching, like he was about to start a sprint. He arched his fingers together over his head and then lifted one leg after the other as he tilted his head to each side. "Whenever you're ready, Simon."

He picked up one leg and started patting his head. "I believe you had released me from the stomach rubbing," he said hopefully.

Anita smiled at him. "Simon said you could stop rubbing your stomach," she agreed. This would be a joke that they always had, she thought happily, before she could remind herself that Frank was a gazillionaire and she made cupcakes. If he won this game, as he seemed determined to do, he'd take her on a date, and…what then?

Was she really his mate? Was any of this real? If she

Simon Said that he should take her over to their sideways table fortress and make love to her in a pile of curtains and tablecloths, would he do it?

What if this was just a silly diversion, like Simon Says itself, and she was just a ridiculous girl building it all up to too much in her own head?

Would there be anything left when the power came on and the roads were cleared and everyone went back to their own lives?

"Can I see the poem you wrote me?" she asked shyly.

Frank ducked his head. "I guess," he said sheepishly. "But I promise I'm no Wordsworth or Rumi."

"Interesting choice of poets," Anita said, glad that she'd at least heard of both of them.

He patted himself, nearly falling over on his one leg to twist for his back pocket. "I don't have it," he said in dismay. "It must have fallen out of my pocket. Maybe it's back at the fort."

He hopped on the one leg all the way back to the ballroom, still patting his head, and Anita took pity on him and squirreled in under his arm to help support him. It didn't feel weird to be up close with him, after their long adventure.

"It's a lot less scary in here now that we know what the ghost was," she said, as they came out of the shadowed hall to the ballroom. "Oh!"

If the view out the windows had been awe-inspiring earlier, it was enchanted now, with the sun starting to set. The clouds had gone from fluffy and slightly gold to rich smeared hues of orange and pink, the sky above fading to purple. The snow-filled valley reflected every color in a soft palette of the most magnificent painter ever.

They had both drawn to a stop, Frank leaning on her just a little. He was a big guy, but he didn't make her feel afraid for a second. He was just exactly as he was supposed to be, somehow.

"Oh, here it is," he said, and he somehow managed to crouch down on the one leg to pick up a tiny promotional notebook with his logo on the cover.

Anita had done enough yoga—it didn't take much!—to know that even for a shifter, his leg must be aching. She ought to take pity on him. She was being entirely too cruel. He'd done every weird thing she told him to without so much as a hesitation, and he hadn't done anything too forward or presumptive, even after he'd leveled that whole mate thing on her.

Especially after the whole mate thing.

She'd said her piece, and he'd taken it for absolute gospel.

And he wrote her poetry.

He'd also crossed it off, Anita discovered, when he reluctantly flipped it open and handed it over to her.

"I'm sorry it's so awful."

"It's not awful," Anita protested.

"You haven't read it yet," Frank pointed out.

> *My flamingo thinks you're swell*
> *To tell the truth, I do as well.*
>
> *You came into my life with snow*
> *You brought with you a happy glow.*
>
> *I know you are my destiny,*
> *Please say you will stay with me.*

Anita read it, making it sing-song in her head. It was silly and sappy and didn't scan perfectly.

"See?" Frank seemed to take her slowness in reading it as proof.

"It is sort of awful," Anita conceded. "But I love it anyway."

It was genuine, like Frank himself. It was straight from his big, beautiful heart.

Harriet, bless her competitive soul, was right about him. He *wasn't* Anita's past, and he *was* really hot, and they *were* totally into each other. She didn't want to waste a perfectly good opportunity, trapped in snowstorm without power, and regret it for the rest of her life.

"You should kiss me," Anita said boldly, and it was delicious to watch Frank's face light up.

She was confused that he didn't lean forward then and close the space between them. He had a really nice mouth and Anita was dying to know if it would feel like she imagined it would against hers.

"You didn't say Simon says," he reminded her.

"Simon says to kiss me," Anita said impatiently.

Frank, still on one leg, still patting his head, reached forward with his other arm and pulled her close. He lost his balance and nearly fell over, but Anita was sturdy and used to accidentally almost knocking people down, so she kept them upright until his mouth was brushing her lips and her whole world went away.

Anita hadn't kissed a lot of people, but she was pretty sure this was an amazing kiss by *any* criteria. He smelled so good and he felt so good, with one arm around her, and when his lips touched hers she felt like she'd been lit on fire.

Good fire, though. Fire blazing through her veins like special effects in a movie. It wasn't scary or overwhelming and she didn't once stop to think that she might be doing it wrong or worry that she would taste bad, she was so happy and excited and he was holding her so close.

Anita didn't realize that she was rubbing herself up against him until he groaned in her mouth and she realized exactly what it was that she was rubbing herself up against.

"I'm sorry," she said breathlessly, pulling back and trying to look anywhere else. Too much. Too forward. Too fast. That's what everyone said about her.

Frank let her go and nearly unbalanced. He was still on one leg and doing a terrible job of patting his own head. "Simon said," he gasped.

Did he only do it because she'd told him to? It was hard to think that he didn't want her the same way she wanted him because of the way he looked at her, and the way he talked about being her mate.

CHAPTER 19

$\mathcal{A}$nita tasted exactly like Frank had expected her to: like cupcakes.

Algae and plankton and saltwater, his flamingo sighed happily.

But it wasn't just the flavor of her, it was the heat of her mouth, and the eagerness of her tongue, and the way her whole body was along for the ride. She was so much person in such a perfect package, and she had a dozen expressions dancing across her sweet face now. How could a complete stranger be so familiar and so comfortable and still feel thrilling and new? He felt like he'd known her forever and just met her, all at once.

He wanted her like he'd never wanted anything else in the world, wanted to capture her in his hands and cage her in his heart forever.

But he knew that it wouldn't work if he trapped her. He had to tame her to his hand, not hide her behind bars.

She licked her lips and smoothed back the hair around her face. Her braid had gotten progressively more wild as the day advanced, and she had curls everywhere. "I'm sorry," she repeated.

"I don't want you to be sorry," Frank said. He wasn't even sure exactly what she was apologizing for, but he knew what he had to do at last.

"Anita," he said, hopping backwards a few feet.

He made sure that she was watching him and stopped patting his head.

Her eyes widened in horror. "I didn't say Simon says!" she warned him, as his foot lowered to the floor. "Oh no!"

Then she looked up at him. "You did that on purpose!" she exclaimed in surprise. Her face fell. "Oh. Oh, you didn't…want to win."

Fix it fix it fix it! Frank's flamingo shrieked.

"I didn't want to win," Frank agreed, stuffing his irritating bird back into his head. "I didn't want you to go out with me because you had to, or felt obligated, just because I am clearly the world's greatest Simon Says player. I want you to go out on a date with me because *you* want to. Not because you're my mate and I'm a billionaire, but because maybe we get along really well, and you want to see where we could go *together.*"

She was silent, which was so ridiculously un-Anita that Frank was a little frightened.

His flamingo hid his metaphorical head under a wing.

"You don't have to," he assured her. "This isn't a trap, and if you tell me you don't want to have anything to do with me, that's what will happen."

She was still quiet.

"I won't call or stalk you," he promised. "I'll never order cupcakes from you again, if that's what you want."

Why wouldn't she talk?? Was he doing this all wrong?

He cleared his throat and started again. "Anita, I want to be frank with you. If you *need a* moment…" He waited to see if she laughed at the joke again, then plowed further on when she didn't, "I'll give you all the moments you need. I'll be patient as it takes. You can have space and time. This is your choice to make."

Could she speak? She was still staring and every so often, she would blink, but her mouth didn't move.

Frank was out of things to say and flailed after what to do next.

Dance? his flamingo suggested hopefully.

Frank didn't have a better idea.

He cleared his throat and bowed to her. "'Miss Townsend,'" he said formally, "'seeing as the Wild and Wet Charity Gala wasn't actually canceled, would you like to dance with me to the music of the lovely orchestra I hired. It sounds like they are starting a waltz.'"

Her smile was so careful that Frank felt a little like he was watching it in slow motion.

"I'd like that," she whispered, and she put one hand into his.

Frank took her gently into his arms, not wanting to spook her.

As sure as his flamingo was of their dancing skills, Frank knew well that he was mediocre-at-best at socially acceptable forms of dancing. He could cut a rug at a wedding where flailing elbows and lots of hugging were expected, but he would never be the surprise winner of a ballroom dancing competition or the star of a reality show that involved footwork. He could do a foxtrot and lead a basic waltz, in a pinch, and he vaguely knew the hand motions to the Macarena.

But without music, completely distracted by the feeling of Anita, who was stiff in his embrace, he was worse than ever.

He tried humming, to give himself a sense of rhythm,

and ended up stuck in a repeating refrain of "I'm a little teapot…" before he collided knees once too often with Anita and she offered, "Do you want me to lead? Or possibly, sing?"

If a flamingo could die of embarrassment, Frank's would have perished on the spot.

"I'm not usually *this* terrible," he said with chagrin.

"I did just make you hop around on one leg for like an hour," Anita pointed out as she drew him in a circle. "Duh duh duh duh duh. Duh duh. Duh duh. Duh duh duh duh duh. Duh duh. Duh duh…"

She led him off in circles that got increasingly wide as they sang the refrain to Blue Danube, over and over again until they were both laughing and dizzy and Frank's flamingo was yodeling happily in his head.

"I love you," he told her, when they had slowed to a more sedate pace. He didn't really mean to, but it just bubbled up out of him. She was close in his arms and they were swaying in place. She had to tip her head to look up at him, but she didn't draw away.

"I'm sorry," he said, seeing the conflicted emotion on her face. "I won't press."

"I…kind of do want you to press," she admitted. "I like you a lot, Frank, and I don't think I'm at code level love yet, but I could sure get there in a hurry. You're the nicest, cutest guy I've ever crushed on, and…you kiss really well."

"Could I kiss you again?" Frank asked.

"Simon says that would be acceptable," Anita said demurely, and her smile was slow enough that it was still in the act of curving up as Frank caught her mouth with his.

It was all a great deal simpler when he was kissing her, that was for sure.

She was fluid in his embrace, soft and strong and sweet,

and she slipped her arms up around his neck like they belonged there.

If their first kiss was magic, this one was wild sorcery.

CHAPTER 20

*A*nita had been trying really hard to be the kind of person who didn't rush into things, but everything about Frank made her want to tear off her own clothing and fling herself at him. She'd spent the entire day wrestling back her intensifying attraction, trying to dampen her own reckless impulses with common sense and life experience.

But the more she was *herself*, the more Frank seemed to like her. He liked all the weird, wild things she came up with, and he didn't seem to think she should always stop talking a sentence earlier. If his hard-on, apparent again, was any indication, he found her as hot as she found him.

And she wanted this guy, in all the dirty-sweet ways that she could imagine. He checked every single one of her boxes for animal desire. He had a body she wanted to climb and wrap her legs around, and he had a face she would have postered on her ceiling so she could go to sleep with him as the last thing she saw before dreaming. His smile was like a magazine cover, and his clever hands made her whimper.

But it was his laugh that made her weak. When he threw back his head and chortled with her, Anita felt like she'd grown wings of her own and could fly.

His second kiss was even hotter than the first one and Anita let her hands wander up so she could feel the muscles in his back and grind herself against his leg and its friend.

His hands wandered, too, from chastely at her waist to take a handful of her ass, and she absolutely loved it, kissing him harder and clawing him accidentally.

"Anita," he said, drawing away for a tantalizing, terrible moment.

"Simon says take me to the penthouse," Anita said, before she could remember her resolve to take things slower and be less forward.

Frank drew away just far enough to shock her by sweeping her up entirely into his arms and marched with her down the back hallway toward the elevator.

They kissed passionately and made out against the wall like horny teenagers there for a long while before they simultaneously realized that pushing the button wasn't working while the power was out.

"The power—" she gasped.

"It's two floors up—" Frank panted.

Frank seemed perfectly willing to lift her back up into his arms and carry her up those stairs. He picked her up and staggered a little because she wasn't that light and he was busy kissing her, besides the fact that he'd been hopping around on one leg for so long.

"Our fort," Anita suggested instead. "It's closer." She was pretty sure that Frank would get her up those two stories without dropping her, but she wasn't sure that *she* would last that long, and she thought it would be more comfortable making love in a pile of tablecloths than it would in a stairwell landing.

Frank said something that might have been a dirty word, or the word *flock*.

"Yes, please," Anita said to either one.

Frank ran into one of the tables by the entrance to the ballroom and nearly dropped Anita. She only screamed a little when she felt herself falling, and Frank caught her at once.

"Sorry," she said. "I'm a screamer. Apparently." The split-second of fear only heightened her excitement.

Frank actually growled as he clutched her possessively. Anita hadn't thought that she'd ever want anyone to be possessive of her again, but this was nothing but delightful. "I love it when you scream," he promised. "Tell me what will make you."

"Oh, options," Anita purred. "Missionary, doggy style? Hold me down, let me ride you? Up against a wall? Sixty-nine? Can we try them all?"

He nearly dropped her again, because he'd gotten them to the fort itself then and Anita wasn't sure how he got over the sideways table, but he finally laid her down in the pile of tablecloths at last and bent to kiss her, hard.

Frank slowed to undress her, and then suddenly paused. "There are condoms in the penthouse," he said between gritted teeth. "I should get one."

"I'm on the pill," Anita said, honestly touched that he'd think of it. "I know that I'm impulsive, so I try to make up for that with common sense."

"You are so amazing," Frank said, and Anita could not have disbelieved him if she had tried. "You are so smart and funny and unexpected and beautiful."

"I should always stop one sentence earlier," she said sheepishly.

"Never stop one sentence earlier," Frank said firmly. "I want to know your every last sentence forever."

CHAPTER 21

Frank was not sure if Anita had been serious about the positions she listed or not, but he was determined to try them all, particularly once he'd gotten her shirt off and freed her breasts from her bra.

They were stupendous breasts. They were round in all the right places, with hard little nipples and tiny freckles over the top where sunlight might hit them in a low-cut shirt.

Even his flamingo was stunned by them. *Breasts…*

Frank might have stayed there the rest of the night, kissing every inch of them, marveling at the way they moved and how they felt when he squeezed them, but Anita was working on getting his shirt off, and her hands on his skin were making him aware of all the other things that he wanted to do with her.

He helped her shuck off his shirt and her breasts against his chest when they kissed again were so perfectly soft and firm and intoxicating that for a while they just sort of rubbed against each other happily while their tongues were busy.

Then her hands were at the button of his jeans and he swiftly drew them both back up to their feet so he could figure out how to get her out of her pants. He forgot about shoes until he got that far, then had to backtrack in order to get them off her feet, both laughing.

Sometimes sex was an awful lot of knowing what went where but not really being sure how to get it there, fumbling together in hunger but not really graceful or comfortable.

Making love to Anita was something else entirely. They were good together from the very start, matched in urgency and readiness, completely compatible and hyper-aware of every touch and reaction. There were no layers of expectation, no wondering if they'd be able to talk afterwards, no awkward surprises. They laughed and kissed and explored each other, gauging reactions and readiness, and needed very few words of direction.

A few whispered *theres* and a couple of *mores* and a hissed *yessssss* and he was buried inside of her where he knew that he belonged, and she was so hot and so tight and so wet that he had to think fixedly about imported titanium screws and machine tolerance to ride out her wave of pleasure and not take his own.

They only got through three of the positions she'd listed, first very safe and vanilla on a bed of curtains, then her on top, with those gorgeous breasts in glorious motion above him. She was as enthusiastic about gratification—his and hers—as she was about everything else she did, and her face, eyes closed in pleasure, mouth parted, was like a painting in the sunset light.

Finally, Frank had her bent over one of the tables on a folded tablecloth, her ass in his hands every bit as alluring as her breasts, her soft cries not quite proving that she was a screamer, but definitely expressing her appreciation. His world narrowed to her sounds, to the feel of being sheathed in her, to her heat, and he lost his last shred of self-control and let himself fall in a glory of release that he'd never imagined.

He wasn't entirely quiet himself, at the end, and they collapsed together and listened to the sounds of their pleasure fade in the echoes to just their panting breath.

"Good thing Harriet didn't stick around," Anita giggled.

She was shivering. The heat was still out, and the hall had continued to get colder. The sun was nearly gone, but Frank could see a wisp of her breath in what was left of the light.

He pulled one of the drapes out from underneath them and flung it over top of them. Unfortunately, this knocked over the box of cupcakes that was still perched on one of the tipped-over tables. The lid popped open and one of them rolled right on top of Anita.

"Let me get that," Frank said nobly, picking up the cupcake and bending to lick the frosting off of her belly. It was one of the yellow cupcakes and tasted like lemon with a hint of mint. "Yum."

Anita was looking at him avidly. "Yum is right," she said, staring at him. "How'd I luck out with a bird like you?"

Frank kissed her and then laughed when Anita licked a smudge of frosting from his nose.

"You're my mate," he said contentedly.

"Crikey," Anita teased. Then her face turned suddenly serious. "Oh, Harriet might have been onto something!" she said, sitting up so fast that she nearly cracked Frank in the face. "Er, sorry."

"What was Harriet onto?" he wanted to know.

"The vinegar sprinkle! I could make a sour lemon

cupcake! A cheek-sucking lemon drop! Not much, of course not as much as she would have used to ruin them, but I could totally market it as a specialty. Oh, and maybe a red hot cinnamon! People love challenging food! I could label the box 'Cupcakes that make you sweat!'" She considered. "Okay, maybe not that. You can help me come up with something better."

"I can't wait," Frank said happily.

Anita sobered. "I suppose we should talk about that, actually."

"Cupcakes that make you sweat?"

She smiled like she was trying not to. "About what happens next. Where do we go from here?"

"The penthouse has blankets. I have a sweater you can wear if you're cold."

"I mean…after this." She wasn't trying not to smile now, her mouth wide and happy in her darling face. "Where would we live? Do you have a mansion or something? I'm not sure my apartment allows flamingos."

"I don't need much," Frank promised. "A yard with some lawn and maybe a wading pool. Flamingos are actually quite resilient. We can stand in boiling or freezing water, drink saltwater, handle acids and toxins. We're like cockroaches; we'll outlast just about everything you throw at us."

Anita giggled helplessly. "Be serious," she said.

"Do I have to?" Frank said. He felt giddy.

Part of it was the afterglow of the greatest sex of his life, but most of it was that he'd found the woman who made him happier than he'd ever imagined possible…and she was willing to be his. "Maybe I can buy this place and we can live here in this table fort. One of those back conference rooms would make a fine nursery."

"It does have a lot of happy memories," Anita agreed.

"Screaming in the bathroom. That time we snubbed Victoria Hennings."

"That time I was in an aerial battle with a trespassing owl," Frank added.

"Did I win the flamingo sculpture?" Anita wanted to know. "I don't think the bidding ever came to an end."

"I'll give it to you," Frank promised. "As a wedding gift."

"It's kind of big," she said, looking across the ballroom at the stage thoughtfully.

Frank snorted. "'That's what she said!'"

They giggled and cuddled together under one of the velvet drapes that didn't have cupcake frosting on it. It was so delicious to have her in his arms, just skin against skin against velvet. They had it tented over their heads, like they were having the greatest sleepover ever.

"Did you mean that?" Anita asked.

"I've always thought that I was quite reasonably endowed," Frank said. "You certainly didn't *sound* disappointed."

"I meant about a wedding," Anita said shyly.

Frank hesitated and his flamingo froze. *Flock?*

"I love you, Anita," he said honestly. "But we don't have to rush into anything you don't want. You can move in with me; I've got a flat downtown with a guest room that can be yours and we can live in dirty sin. Or you can keep your apartment if you like. Or we can rent something in between. I'm not worried about time, or cost, or judgmental relatives, or gossip columns. I only care that you're happy and feel safe and know that I love you. If you want me to prove it with a ring, I will."

He couldn't really see Anita under the dark drapery, but he could feel her snuggle closer and give a great sigh of contentment.

Snuggle! his flamingo said happily.

After a moment, Anita lifted her head, knocking it into his chin the way she had when she woke up. "Er, sorry. Still graceless."

"Still Frank," he replied.

She giggled. "You are. You are perfectly Frank. And I love you, I think, and I'm not quite ready for wedding bells but I wouldn't say no to a ring."

"I'll make you one!" Frank declared. "Do you want a clockwork ring with a tiny little pink diamond flamingo in it?"

Flock!

There was no way that he could resist kissing her then, cradling her into his arms and leaning her back so that he could feel all of her against all of him.

A sudden pop drove them back up to upright. "Did you hear someone?" Anita asked, her arms tighter around him now.

Frank eased the curtain-tent back and squinted into unexpected brightness. "The power is back on!"

The sounds of lights and ventilation were loud after the post-storm silence, and Frank felt a little lost and off balance. He and Anita got to their feet. Neither of them had a stitch of clothing on and Anita's reflection in the window was like a curvy little goddess. She was shivering. "I bet the elevator works now," she suggested hopefully.

Frank thought that this was a great plan. "It might take a little while, but I bet there will be warm water soon, and we can have hot showers and airplane nuts in my penthouse."

"'Airplane nuts, you say?'" Anita had slipped back into her snotty voice. She stooped to gather up her clothing. "'I say, Frank Wilson, you do throw a very fine all-day charity event and sleepover.'"

"The sleepover part is the best part," he promised.

"As long as there are blankets on that bed," Anita said, shivering in earnest now.

"I will keep you warm," Frank promised. "For the rest of my life, I will keep you warm." He grabbed one of the tablecloths to swirl around them and helped her vault over the tipped-over table.

Snuggle! his flamingo yodeled, as they hurried for the elevator, which obediently came at their command this time. The hallways were very bright and different now that they were lit again, but the timing was good, because it was almost full dark outside.

"'I suggest that you escort me to the penthouse, Mr. Wilson,'" Anita commanded as the elevator doors opened for them.

"'I shall do exactly that, Miss Townsend,'" Frank said.

Flock! Flock! Flock! his flamingo cried in joy.

EPILOGUE

*H*arriet landed on her balcony, shifted, and limped to the sliding door she'd left unlocked. She had to wade through a rather shocking amount of snow and wrench on the door much harder than usual, because ice had formed at all the edges.

She wrestled it shut again, and snow fell in all over the carpet and started to melt.

Harriet was too tired and sore to deal with it and she kicked off her silver shoes and went to the bathroom to start a well-deserved bath. At least her apartment had power, though the blinking light above the kitchen stove suggested it had been out.

Frank had gotten a good strike with his beak at her leg while they were fighting, and Anita had just about crushed her in that last tackle. Harriet probably would have made a better showing in the battle if she hadn't foolishly strained her wing flying to a useless *canceled* charity event.

That stupid bubbly baker and her ridiculous flamingo billionaire beau.

She didn't suppose that it was really their fault that her

grand plan had failed because of the unexpected snow-storm. They were pretty cute…and so *clueless*. They had bought into her 'sabotage the cupcakes' story without a single doubt or hesitation.

Anita had even *hugged* her.

The bathroom was starting to steam as Harriet wriggled out of her fancy dress, hanging it with the other high end frocks that she'd accumulated. She paused to run her fingers down a velvet black gown.

It was an impressive collection for a simple baker.

But it was perfectly in character for a jewel thief.

Harriet returned to the bathroom to pile her hair up onto her head and check the temperature of the water. The tub was half full.

Oh, Harriet had certainly intended to ruin Anita's cupcakes, and she hadn't feigned *all* of her sympathy once they'd actually met and her rival baker proved to be a ridiculous rube. A ridiculous rube with a sense of humor and whimsy that Harriet found herself reluctantly *liking*. And it wasn't really Anita's fault that she made better cupcakes and had an actual business plan that involved selling them.

Harriet's bakeries were just a front for the money that she made stealing jewels and art, the perfect, innocent excuse for laundering the cash from her crimes and heists. Her cupcakes were mediocre and she knew it, but if sales fell off too obviously, her cover was blown.

The Wet and Wild Charity Gala and Auction was a chance for the city's fanciest, frocked-up fellows to come out showing off their wealth and good fortune by wearing it around their necks and at their wrists and ears as they pledged pittances to worthy causes.

Harriet had planned to arrive early and hide until the event was under way, then mingle as one of the guests, carefully relieving them of a choice selection of the easiest pieces to fence. She was very talented at evaluating risk and reward, and she had a half dozen acts in her pocket.

Oh, you've lost an earring, let me help you find it! and *That's such a lovely necklace, tell me all about it* while she lifted their bracelets or gently released diamonds from their settings. She made sure that her brilliant red hair (a temporary dye over her more usual strawberry blonde that would wash out in a few days) was more memorable than her face, and she was an expert at deflection.

If they recalled her with suspicion when they eventually discovered their loss, there was nothing to trace back to her. She wasn't on the guest list, and Patty Cakes hadn't even gotten the contract for the event!

Tainting Anita's cupcakes would have acted as a diversion, a topic of conversation, and taken her pseudo-rival out of the picture, all in one neat package.

Once she'd forced a little more charity than they had in mind, she'd be off on the wing with her prizes, and richer by a lot.

Instead, she'd had to witness the world's most awkward courtship and come away completely empty-handed.

Harriet liked things hot or cold. Drinking water should be a degree from freezing and bath water should be a degree from boiling alive. That was the bath she stepped into now, hissing a little as she slipped gingerly down into it until she was completely covered up to her chin.

Slowly, her tense body began to relax and Harriet wadded a washcloth up to lean her head against.

She had a great life and a thrilling career. She had no reason to be jealous of someone like Anita, who was silly and boring. So what if Frank was a well-built billionaire who'd known at once that she was his mate?

Harriet hadn't intended to eavesdrop, but an owl's

hearing was almost as keen as their eyesight and it had been hard to miss their exuberant exchanges in the quiet hall.

It bothered her exactly how much she longed for the kind of connection that she'd witnessed. She was tough and independent…and she came home to a house that was echoing empty.

Was it possible that there was someone out there who could fill that emptiness? Someone for *her*?

She blew impatient ripples on the surface of the water.

Who? her owl asked wistfully.

Who indeed.

A NOTE FROM ELVA BIRCH

I am not writing the next book with Tobias and Harriet. I am not writing the gnome puns or the jewel heists. I am definitely not writing the Christmas Charity Gala at Wilson Kinetic or the cupcake war that happens there. I'm not possibly researching new gnome jokes or owl facts… and you should certainly not subscribe to my newsletter or join my Reader's Retreat on Facebook in order to get sneak previews and snippets of this book I'm not actually writing…

Your reviews are very much appreciated; I read them all and they help other readers decide whether or not to buy my books! A huge thank you to all of my fabulous beta readers and copy editors; any errors that remain are entirely my own. If you find typos — or you'd just like share your thoughts with me! — please feel free to email me at elvaherself@elvabirch.com.

I also write under other pen names—keep reading for information about my other available titles…

MORE BY ELVA BIRCH

Want some more extra short stories, including a Shifting Sands Resort ménage? Join my mailing list for sneak previews, extras, bonus stories, and more, or join my Reader's Retreat on Facebook!

~

A Day Care for Shifters: A hot new full-length series about adorable shifter kids and their struggling single parents in a town full of mystery and surprise. Start the series with Wolf's Instinct, when Addison comes to Nickel City to take a job at a very special day care and finds a family to belong to. A gentle ice-cream-straight-from-the-container escape. Sweet and sizzling!

The Royal Dragons of Alaska: A fascinating alternate world where Alaska is ruled by secret dragon shifters. Adventure, romance, and humor! Reluctant royalty, relentless enemies…dogs, camping, and magic! Start with The Dragon Prince of Alaska.

Suddenly Shifters: A hilarious series of novellas, serials, and shorts set in the small town of Anders Canyon, where something (in the water?) is making ordinary citizens turn into shifters. Start with Something in the Water!

Lawn Ornament Shifters: The series that was only supposed to be a joke, this is a collection of short, ridiculous romances featuring unusual shifters, myths, and magic. Cross-your-legs funny and full of heart! Start with The Flamingo's Fated Mate!

Birch Hearts: An enchanting collection of short stories and novellas. Unconstrained by theme or setting, each short read has romance, magic, and heart, with a satisfying conclusion. And always, the impossible and irresistible. Start with a sampler plate in Prompted 2 for fourteen pieces of sweet-to-sizzling flash fiction, or dive in with the novella, Better Half - which you can get free for joining my mailing list!

Shifting Sands Resort: A complete ten-book series—plus two collections of shorts. This is a sizzling shifter romance set at a tropical island resort. Each book stands alone but connects into a great mystery with a thrilling conclusion. Start with Tropical Tiger Spy or dive in to the Omnibus edition, with all of the novels, short stories, and novellas in my preferred reading order! This series crosses over with *Shifter Kingdom* and *Fire and Rescue Shifters*.

≈

Fae Shifter Knights: A complete four-book fantasy portal romp, with cute pets and swoon-worthy knights stuck in a world of wonders like refrigerators and ham sandwiches. Start with Dragon of Glass!

≈

Green Valley Shifters: A sweet, small town series with single dads, secret shifters, sweet kids, and spinsters. Lowperil and steamy! Standalone books where you can revisit your favorite characters—this series is also complete! Start with Dancing Barefoot! This series crosses over with Virtue Shifters.

BEHIND THE SCENES

What is Patreon?

Patreon is a site where readers and fans can support creators with monthly subscriptions.

At my Patreon, I have tiers with early rough drafts of my books, flash fiction, coloring pages, signed and sketched paperbacks, exclusive swag, original artwork, photographs…and so much more! Every month is a little different, and there is a price for every budget. Patreon allows me to do projects that aren't very commercial and makes my income stream a little less unpredictable. It also gives me a place to connect with my fans!

Come find out what's going on behind the scenes and keep me creating at Patreon! patreon.com/ellenmillion

www.ingramcontent.com/pod-product-compliance
Lightning Source LLC
Chambersburg PA
CBHW072054150726
47999CB00005B/1766